MARY
ANN'S
ANGELS

MARY ANN'S ANGELS

CATHERINE COOKSON

c. 1

WILLIAM MORROW AND COMPANY, INC.

NEW YORK   1978

Library of Congress Catalog Card Number   78-53413

ISBN 0-688-03317-2

Printed in the United States of America.

First Edition

1   2   3   4   5   6   7   8   9   10

TO MAM
MY
MOTHER-IN-LAW

MARY
ANN'S
ANGELS

I

"If he can talk, why doesn't he, Rose Mary Boyle?"

"'Cos he doesn't want to, Annabel Morton."

The two six-year-olds stared at each other, eyes wide, nostrils dilated. Their lips spread away from their teeth, they had all the appearance of two caged circus animals dressed up in human guise for the occasion.

"My mam says he's dumb."

"Your mam's barmy."

Again, wide eyes, quivering nostrils and stretched lips, and a waiting period, during which the subject of their conversation, one hand held firmly in that of his twin, gazed alternately at the two combatants. He was fair-haired, round-faced, with dark blue eyes, and his expression was puzzling, for it could have been described as vacant, yet again it could have been described as calculating.

"He spoke the day, an' if your ears hadn't been full of muck, you'd have heard him."

The fray was reopened. Rose Mary turned to her brother and bounced her head towards him, whereupon he stared back at her for a moment, then looked towards their opponent again.

"He made a funny sound, that's all he did, when he was eating his dinner."

"He didn't make a funny sound, he said 'HOT'."

"He didn't, he said 'ugh!' Like a pig makes."

Rose Mary's right, and working arm, throwing itself instinctively outwards, almost lifted David from the ground, and by the time he had relinquished his hold of her hand and regained his balance, with her help, Annabel Morton had put a considerable distance between them. And from this distance she made a stand. "Dumb David!" she called. Then added, "And

7

Rose Mary, pain-in-the-neck, Boyle." And if this wasn't enough she went as far as to mis-spell Boyle. "B-O-I-L!" she screamed at the limit of her lungs.

"Now, now, now." There loomed over Annabel the tall, thin figure of her teacher, Miss Plum.

Rose Mary, her hand again holding David's, watched Miss Plum as she reprimanded that awful Annabel Morton. Oh, she hoped she got kept in the morrow. Oh, she did. And Miss Plum was nice, after all she was nice. Oh, she was.

Now Miss Plum was advancing towards her, and Rose Mary greeted her with uplifted face, over which was spread a smile, the like that had in the past been called angelic . . . by people viewing it for the first time. Miss Plum had never made that mistake. She looked down on Rose Mary now and, her finger wagging near her nose, she said, "I don't want to hear, Rose Mary, I don't want to hear. And you should be on your way home."

"But Miss Pl——"

"No, not another word. Away with you now."

Rose Mary turned round abruptly, and her twin had his eyes wrenched from Miss Plum and was jerked into step by his sister's side, and only because she was grasping his hand firmly could he keep up with her. His legs were plump, and although he was older than his sister by five minutes his speed was geared to about half hers. But of necessity, perhaps out of instinctive urge for preservation, he had learned to put on a brake against her speed. He did it now by throwing himself backwards and resting on his heels.

Rose Mary came to a stop. She looked at him and said, "Miss Plum! Four-eyed, goggle-mug Plum. Her head's like Lees's clock." Whereupon David laughed a high appreciative laugh, for as everybody in Felling knew, even the works in Lees's clock were made of wood.

Rose Mary now joined her laugh to her brother's. Then pulling him to her side, she walked at a slower pace down Stewart Terrace, and as she walked, her whole mien sober now, she thought, "It must be made of wood else she'd be able to make him talk. There must be something that would make him talk,

8

more than one—unintelligible to others—word at a time. Yes, there must be something. But what?"

When she felt a sharp tug on her hand she realized she had almost passed the point where they crossed over to get the bus, but David hadn't. She looked at him in admiration, a grin splitting her pert face. "There, you see," she addressed an adversary known only to herself. "He's all right, you see. I nearly didn't cross over, but he was all there." She jerked her head at the adversary, then gripping David's hand more tightly, she crossed over the road and went towards the bus stop.

The bus conductor, assisting them upwards with a hand on each of their shoulders, said, "Come on, you Siamese twins you. And don't you have so much to say, young fellow-me-lad." He pushed David playfully in the back. "And now I want none of your cheek," he admonished him with a very thick index finger as David hoisted himself on to a seat.

David grinned broadly at the conductor, and Rose Mary, handing him their passes, said, "You back then?"

"Well, if I'm not," said the conductor, straightening up, "somebody's havin' a fine game." Then bending down to her again, he asked under his breath, "No talkie-talkie?"

Rose Mary shook her head.

"Shame."

They both now looked at David.

"Aw well." The conductor ruffled David's hair. "Don't you worry, young chap, you're all there."

When the conductor had passed down the bus Rose Mary and David exchanged glances, and to her glance Rose Mary added a small inclination of the head. The bus conductor was a nice man, he knew that their David was all there.

The bus stopped on the long, bare, main road, bare that is except for traffic, and right at the top end of their side road. Rose Mary and David stood gazing at the conductor where he stood on the platform until he was lost to their sight, then hand in hand they ran up the lane that lay between two fields, and to home.

The first sight they got of home was of two petrol pumps, around which lay a curved line of whitewashed stones. The line

9

was terminated at each end by green tubs which were now full of wallflowers, and to the right-hand side of the pumps and some distance behind them, there stood their home. Their wonderful, wonderful home. At least it was to Rose Mary; David, as yet, had not expressed any views about it.

The house itself was perched on top of what looked like a shop, because the front of the ground floor was taken up by a large plate-glass window and was actually the showroom to the garage. But at present it was empty. Next to the house was a low building with a door and one window, and above the door was a board which read simply: FELL GARAGE: C. BOYLE, Proprietor. Below this, above the door frame, was another slim board with the single word "OFFICE" written on it. To the side of the office was a large barn-like structure, the garage itself, and inside, and leaving it looking almost empty, were three cars. One car stood on its own, a 1950 Rover, which was polished to a gleaming sheen. The other cars were undergoing repairs, and under each of them someone was at work.

"Hello, Dad." Rose Mary, still pulling David with her, dashed up to the man who was lying on his back half underneath the first car, and for answer, Corny kicked one leg in the air, and when they knelt down on the ground by his side to get a better look at him his muffled yell came at them, "Get up out of that, you'll be all oil. Get up with you."

By the time he had edged himself from underneath the car, they were on their feet, grinning at him.

"Hello there." He looked down on them. "Had a nice day?"

"Ah-ha." Rose Mary jerked her chin up at him, then brought her head down to a level position and a soberness to her face, before adding, "Well, except for Annabel Morton. She's a pig."

"Oh. What's she done now?" Corny was wiping his greasy hands with a mutton cloth.

"Here." His daughter beckoned his distant head down to hers, and when his ear was level with her mouth, she whispered, "She said he couldn't talk."

As Corny straightened himself up and looked down at his daughter, who was his wife in miniature, he wanted to say,

"Well she's right, isn't she?" but that would never do, so he said, "She doesn't know what she's talking about."

"An' I told her, an' I told her that."

"And what did she say?"

Rose Mary, picking up David's hand, now turned him about, and glancing over her shoulder at her father, said flatly, "She called me pain-in-the-neck Boyle."

There came a great roar of laughter, but not from her dad. It came from behind the other car, and she yelled at it, "Aw, you Jimmy!" before dashing out of the garage, along the cement walk, around the back of the house—no going in the front way, except for company—and up the stairs, still dragging David with her. And from here she shouted, "Mam. Mam. We're here, Mam."

"Is that my angels?"

As they burst on to the top landing, Mary Ann came out of the kitchen and, stooping over them, enfolded them in her arms, hugging them to her.

"Oh, Mam." Rose Mary sniffed. "You been bakin'? What you been bakin'?"

"Apple tarts, scones, tea-cakes."

"Ooh! Mam. Coo, I'm hungry, starvin'. So's David."

Mary Ann, still on her hunkers, looked at her son, and, a smile seeping from her face, she said to him quietly, "Are you hungry, David?"

The light in the depths of David's eyes deepened, his round, button-shaped mouth spread wide as he stared back at his mother.

"Say, 'Yes, Mam'."

For answer David made a sound in his throat and fell against her, and, putting her hand on the back of his head she pressed it to her, and over it she looked at her daughter. And Rose Mary returned her glance, soft with understanding.

Now Mary Ann, pushing them both before her, said, "Go and get your playthings on. Hang your coats up. And Rose Mary. . . ." When her daughter turned towards her she said slowly, "Rose Mary, let David take his own things off and put his playthings on."

"But Mam . . ."

"Rose Mary, now do as I say, that's a good girl. Go on now, and I'll butter a tea-cake to keep you going until teatime."

When they had gone into their room Mary Ann stood looking down at her hands. They were working one against the other, making a harsh sound; the action made her separate them as if she was throwing something off.

She was in the kitchen again when her daughter's voice came to her from the little room across the landing, saying, "I hate Miss Plum, Mam."

"I thought you liked Miss Plum, I thought she was your favourite teacher?"

"She's not, I hate her. She's a pig."

"Now I've told you about calling people pigs, haven't I?"

"Well, she is, Mam."

"What did she do?"

"She wouldn't let me talk."

Mary Ann, about to lay the tea cloth over the table under the window, put her hand over her mouth to suppress her laughter. It was as if she had gone back down the years and was listening to herself.

"Mam."

"Yes?"

"David drew a lovely donkey the day, with me on its back."

"Oh, that's wonderful. Have you brought it home?"

"No. Miss Plum said it was good, and she pinned it on the wall."

"Oh, that's marvellous." Mary Ann swung the cloth across the table, then paused and looked down, over the garden behind the garage, on to the waste land, and she thought, "I'm blessed. I'm doubly blessed. He'll talk one day. Please God, he'll talk one day."

"We're ready." They were standing in the doorway when she turned round to them.

"Come and have your tea-cakes."

"Can't we take them out with us?"

"Yes, if you like. . . . Did David change himself?"

Rose Mary's brows went upwards, and her eyelids came down

slowly twice before she said, "I helped button him up, that's all."

Mary Ann handed them the tea-cakes, and they turned from her and ran across the landing and down the back stairs, and as she listened to Rose Mary, her voice high now, talking to her brother telling him what games they were going to play, she was back in the surgery this time last week looking at the doctor across the desk. He was smiling complacently and telling her in effect to do the same. "Not to worry, not to worry," he said. "Half his trouble, I think, is his sister. He doesn't talk because there's no real necessity, she's always done it for him. But don't worry, he's not mental, or anything like that. He'll likely start all of a sudden, and then you won't be able to keep him quiet." And he had added that he didn't see much point at present in separating them.

Separate them? As if she would ever dream of separating them; it would be like cutting off one of their arms. Separate them, indeed. If David's power of speech would come only by separating them, then he would remain dumb. On that point she was firm. No matter what Corny said. . . .

It was half-past five when Corny came upstairs. The seven years during which he had been the owner of a garage, a married man, and the father of two children had aged him. The boy, Corny, was no more. The man, Corny, was a six-foot-two, tough-looking individual, with a pair of fine, deep blue eyes in an otherwise plain face. But his plain features were given a particular charm when he smiled or grinned. To Mary Ann he was still irresistible, yet there were times when even their Creator could not have been blamed for having his doubts as to their love for each other.

"Anything new?" She mashed the tea as she spoke.

"Thompson's satisfied with the repairs."

"Did he pay you?"

"Yes, in cash, and gave me ten bob extra."

"Oh, good." She turned and smiled at him.

"Hungry?"

"So, so."

"Give them a shout."

13

Corny went to the window and, opening it, called, "Tea up."
The thin voice of Rose Mary came back to him, crying, "Wait a minute, Dad, he's nearly finished."

"What are they up to over there?"

"They were digging a hole when I last looked," said Mary Ann.

"Digging a hole?" said Corny, screwing up his eyes. "They're piling up stones on top of something. . . . Come along this minute. Do you hear me?"

"Comin', comin'."

A few minutes later, as they came scampering up the stairs, Mary Ann called to them, "Go and wash your hands first, and take your coats off."

Tea was poured out and Corny was seated at the head of the little table when the children entered the room. "What were you up to over there?" He smiled at Rose Mary as he spoke.

"David made a grave," she said, hitching herself on to her seat.

Mary Ann turned swiftly from the stove and looked at her daughter. "A grave?" she said. "What for?"

"To bury Annabel Morton and Miss Plum in."

"Rose Mary!" There was a strong reprimand in Mary Ann's voice. "How could you."

"But I didn't, Mam, he did it hisself."

"He couldn't do it himself, child." Mary Ann leaned across the table and addressed her daughter pointedly, and Rose Mary, her lips now trembling, said, "But he did, Mam." Then turning to David, she said, "Didn't you, David?"

David smiled at her; he smiled at his mother; then smiled at his father. And Corny, holding his son's gaze, said quietly, "You dug a grave, David?"

David remained staring, unblinking.

"You dug a grave, David, and put Miss Plum and Annabel Morton in?"

Still the unblinking stare, which left Corny baffled and not a little annoyed. Turning to his daughter, he now asked her quietly, "How do you know it was Miss Plum and this Annabel Morton?"

"'Cos he took a picture out of my book, the Bantam family, where the mammy wears glasses like Miss Plum."

"And he put that in the hole?" asked Corny, still quietly. Rose Mary nodded.

"And what did he put in for . . . for Annabel Morton?"

"A bit out of the funnies, 'The One Tooth Terror', 'cos Annabel Morton's got stick-out teeth with a band on."

Corny put his elbow on the table and rubbed his hand hard over his face before again looking at his daughter and saying, "And who told him to dig the grave and bury the pictures in it?"

"I didn't, Dad."

"Rose Mary!" The name was a threat now, and Rose Mary's lips trembled visibly, and she said again in a tiny squeaking voice, "I didn't, Dad, I'm tellin' the truth I am. He thought it all up for hisself, he did."

"You're going to instruction for confession on Thursday, Rose Mary; what will you tell Father Carey?"

"Not that, Dad, not that, 'cos I didn't."

"Well, how did you know it was a grave?"

"I don't know, Dad, I don't know." The tears were on her lashes now.

"Corny." Mary Ann's voice was low, and it, too, was trembling, but Corny, without looking at her, waved her to silence and went on, "Did he tell you it was Miss Plum and Annabel Morton?"

"No, Dad."

"You just knew?"

"Yes, Dad."

"How?"

"'Cos he dug a long hole and put the pictures in the bottom and covered them up, like when they put people in the ground in Longfields."

"Have you ever seen anyone being put in the ground in Longfields?"

"Corny." Mary Ann's voice was high now, but still he waved her to silence.

"Yes, and everybody was cryin'. . . ."

Corny lowered his eyes, then said, "And you didn't tell David to do this?"

15

"No, Dad. I was diggin' my garden, putting in the seeds you gave me, when I saw him diggin' a long hole. Then he ran back to the shed where all our old books an' things are and he came back with the pictures."

Once more Corny and David were looking at each other. David's lips were closed, gently closed, his eyes were dark and bright, and if he hadn't been a six-year-old child, a retarded six-year-old child, a supposedly retarded six-year-old child to Corny's mind, he would have sworn that there was a twinkle of amusement in the eyes gazing innocently into his. He rose from the table, pushing his chair back, and went out of the room, and Mary Ann, looking from one to the other of the children, said quickly, "Get on with your teas. No chatter now, get on with your teas." And then she followed her husband.

Corny was expecting her, for when she went into the bedroom he rounded on her immediately, and with his arm extended down towards her he wagged his hand in her face, saying, "It's as I've said before, that little bloke's laughing at us, he's having us on a string."

"Stop talking about your son as that bloke, will you, Corny; it's as if he didn't belong to you."

"Look, I'm not going to be made a fool of by a nipper of six, no matter what you say. As I said before, if he was on his own for a time he would talk all right. Send him to the farm for a few weeks and he'll come back yelling his head off."

"No, no; they can't be separated, they mustn't be separated. And the doctor said so. It's inhuman. I don't know how you can stand there and say such a thing. He's your son, but the way you talk you'd imagine he didn't belong to you."

"He's my son all right, and I want him as a son, and not as the shadow of Rose Mary. If he can think up that grave business and put the teacher and the Morton child into it because they had upset Rose Mary, he's got it up top all right. The only reason he's not talking is because he finds it easier not to. And mark you this." His finger was jabbing at her again. "He thinks it funnier not to. . . . That bloke. . . . All right, all right, all right, THAT CHILD. Well, that child is laughing up his sleeve at us, let me tell you."

"Don't be so silly. A child of six. . . . Huh!"

"Six, you say. Sometimes I think he's sixty. I believe he's an old soul in a young body."

"Oh, Corny." Mary Ann's voice was derisive now, and she closed her eyes giving emphasis to her opinion on this particular subject. "You've been reading again."

"Never mind about reading, I mean what I say, and as I've said before, if those two are separated that boy'll talk, and that's just what I'm . . ."

"Well, you try it." Mary Ann drew herself up to the limit of her five feet as she interrupted him, and, her face now red and straight, she said under her breath, "You separate them and you know what I'll do . . . I'll go home."

As soon as it was out she knew she had made a grave mistake. In her husband were a number of sensitive spots, which she had learnt it was better to by-pass, and now she had jumped on one with both feet, and she watched the pain she had caused, tightening his muscles and bringing his mouth to that hard line which she hated.

"This is your home, Mary Ann, I've told you before. These four rooms are your home. You chose them with your eyes open. The place that you've just referred to is the house where your parents live, the home of your children's grandparents, but this . . ." He took his fist and brought it down with a bang on the corner post of the wooden bed. "This is your home."

"Oh, Corny." It was a faint whisper. "I'm sorry. You know I didn't mean it."

"You've said it before."

"But I didn't mean it. I never mean it." She moved close to him and leant her head against his unyielding chest, and, putting her arms about him, she said, "I'm sorry. Hold . . . hold me tight."

It was a few minutes before Corny responded to the plea in her voice. Then, his arms going about her, he said stiffly, "I'll get you a better house, never you fear. One of these days I'll build you a house, and right here. But in the meantime, don't look down on this . . ."

"Oh, Corny." She had her head strained back gazing up at him and protesting, "I don't, I don't. Oh that's not fair, you know I don't."

"I don't know you don't, I know nothing of the sort, because you're always breaking your neck to visit the farm."

"Well, so are you. Look at the Sundays I've wanted to stay put, but it's been you who's said, 'Let's go over. If we don't they'll wonder. And they want to see the bairns!' You've said that time and again."

"I've said it because I knew you wanted to go. All right, let's forget it." He took her elfin face between his two big hands, and after gazing at it for a moment he said below his breath, "Oh, Mary Ann." Then pulling her close to him, he moved his hand over her hair, saying, "Aw, I want to give you things . . . the lot, and it irks me when I go to the farm and everybody looks prosperous. Your da and ma, Michael and Sarah, Tony and Lettice."

"Aw, now, Corny, that's not fair." She was bristling again. "It isn't all clover for Tony and Lettice living with Mr. Lord. As for me ma and da looking prosperous. Well, after the way they've struggled. And as for our Michael and Sarah, we could have had a better place than them if . . ." Mary Ann suddenly found her words cut off by Corny's hand being placed firmly but gently across her mouth.

"I'll say it for you." Corny was speaking slowly. "If I'd taken the old man's offer and let him set me up with the Baxter garage, we'd have been on easy street. That's what you were getting at, isn't it? But I've told you before I'd rather eat bread and dripping and be me own boss. I'm daft I know, do-lally-tap, up the pole, the lot, I know, but that's the way I'm made. And again I say, you knew what you were taking on, didn't you?"

He took his hand slowly away from her mouth, and with his arms by his sides now he stood looking at her, and she at him. Then she smiled up at him, a loving little smile, as she said, "And I've told you this afore, Corny Boyle. You're a big pig-headed, stubborn, conceited lump of . . ."

"You forgot the bumptious. . . ."

18

Suddenly they were laughing, and he grabbed her up and swung her round as if she, too, was a child.

"Eeh! stop it, man, you'll have the things over." She thumped him on the chest, and as he plonked her down on the side of the bed there came to them from directly below the wailing note of a trombone.

The sound seemed to prevent Mary Ann from overbalancing. Looking up at Corny, she screwed her face up as she exclaimed, "Oh, no! No!"

"Look." He bent his long length down to her. "It's only for half-an-hour. I told him he could after he had finished the job and before the bairns had gone to bed. And think back, Mary Ann, think back. Remember when I hadn't any place to practice me cornet, who took pity on me?" He flicked her chin with his forefinger and thumb.

"But that's a dreadful sound, he knows nothing about it."

"So was my cornet."

"Aw, it wasn't." She pushed him aside as she got to her feet. "You could always play, you were a natural. But Jimmy. Why doesn't he stick to his guitar, he isn't bad at that?"

"They're trying to make the group different, introducing a trombone and a flute into it."

"Well, why didn't he pick the flute?" She put her fingers in her ears as a shrill wobbling note penetrated the floor-boards. "Oh, let's get into the other room. Not that it will be much better there."

As they entered the kitchen Rose Mary turned excitedly from the table, crying, "Jimmy's playing his horn, Mam."

"Yes, dear, I can hear. Have you finished your tea?"

"Nearly, Mam. David wants some cheese."

"David can't have any cheese, I've told you it upset his stomach before. He's got an egg and . . ." She bent over her son and looked down into the empty egg-cup, saying, "Oh, you've eaten your egg, that's a good boy. But where's the shell?" She turned her eyes to her daughter, and Rose Mary, looking down at her plate, said quietly, "I think he threw it in the fire, he sometimes does. But he'd like some cheese, he's still hungry."

19

"Now, Rose Mary, don't keep it up. I've told you he can't have any cheese."

"I've had some cheese."

"Oh." Mary Ann closed her eyes and, refusing to be drawn into a fruitless argument, took her seat at the table, only to bring her shoulders hunching up and her head down as an extra long wail from the trombone filled the room.

When it died away and she straightened herself up it was to see her daughter convulsed with laughter. David, too, was laughing, his deep, throaty, infectious chuckle. She was feigning annoyance, saying, "It's all right for you to laugh," when she saw Corny standing behind David's chair. He was motioning to her with his head, and so, quietly, she rose from the table and walked to his side and stood behind the children, and following her husband's eyes her gaze was directed to the pocket in her son's corduroy breeches. The pocket was distended, showing the top of a brown egg.

As they exchanged glances, she wanted to laugh, but it was no laughing matter. This wasn't the first time that food had been stuffed into her son's pockets, or up his jumper; it had even found its way into the chest of drawers. She was about to lift her hand to touch David when a warning movement from Corny stopped her. The movement said, leave this to me. Quietly she walked to her seat and Corny, taking his seat, drew his son's attention to him by saying, "David."

David turned his laughing face towards his father.

"Did you eat the egg that Mam give you for your tea?"

The smile slid from David's face, the eyes widened into innocence, the moist lips parted, and he bestowed on his father a look which said he didn't understand.

"Dad. Dad, he tried . . ."

"Rose Mary!" Without moving a muscle of his face Corny's eyes slid to his daughter. "Remember what I told you about telling lies. Now be quiet." The eyes turned on his son once again. "Where's the egg you had for your tea, David?"

Still no movement from David. Still the innocent look. Now Corny held out his hand. He laid it on the table in front of his son and said quietly, "Give it to me."

David's eyelids didn't flicker, but his small hand moved down towards his trouser pocket, then came upwards again, holding the egg. It took up a position about eight inches above Corny's hand, and there remained absolutely still.

"Give me the egg, David." Corny's voice was quiet and level.

And David gave his father the egg, his little fist pressed into the softly-boiled egg crushing the shell. As the yoke dripped on to Corny's fingers he smacked at his son's hand, knocking the crushed egg flying across the table, to splatter itself over the stove. Then almost in one movement he had David dangling by the breeches as if he was a hold-all, and with his free hand he lathered his behind.

David's screams now rent the air and vied with the screeches of the trombone and the crying of Rose Mary as she yelled, "Oh, Dad, don't. Oh don't hit David. Don't. Don't."

Mary Ann wanted to say the same thing, "Don't hit David. Don't," but David had to be smacked. Quickly, she thrust Rose Mary from the room, saying, "Stay there. . . . Now stay." And turning to Corny, she cried, "That's enough. That's enough."

After the first slap of anger she knew that Corny hadn't belaboured David as he could have done. It was only during these past few months that he had smacked his son, and although she knew it had to be done and the boy deserved it the process tore her to shreds.

She wanted to go to David now and gather him up from the big chair where he was crouched and into her arms, and pet him and mother him, but that would never do. She took him by the hand and drew him to his feet, saying, "Go into the bathroom and get your things off."

Outside the door, Rose Mary was waiting. She exchanged a look with her mother; then, putting her arms about her brother, she almost carried him, still sobbing, to the bathroom.

When Mary Ann returned to the room Corny said immediately, "Now don't say to me that I shouldn't have done that." She looked at him and saw that his face was white and strained, she saw that he was upset more than usual, and she could understand this. The defiance of his son, the indignity of the egg being

21

squashed on to his fingers, and having to thrash the child had upset him, for he loved the boy. About his feelings for his son, she had once analysed them to herself by saying that he was crazy about Rose Mary but he loved David.

Everything seemed to have changed this last year, to have got worse over the past few months. At times she thought it was as Corny said, David had it all up top and he was trying something on. And this was borne out by the incident just now, for even she had to admit it appeared calculated.

Another blast from the trombone penetrating the room, she flew to the window, thrust it open and, leaning out, she cried, "Jimmy! Jimmy, will you stop that racket!"

"What, Mrs. Boyle. . . . Eh?"

She was now looking down on the long lugubrious face of Corny's young assistant, Jimmy McFarlane. Jimmy was seventeen. He was car mad, motor-cycle mad and group mad, in fact Mary Ann would say Jimmy was mad altogether, but he was a hard worker, likeable and good tempered. Apart from all that, he was all they could afford in the way of help.

"Sorry, Mrs. Boyle, is it disturbin' you? Is the bairns abed?"

"They're just going, Jimmy, but . . . but give it a rest for to-night at any rate, will you?"

"O.K., Mrs. Boyle." Jimmy's voice did not show his disappointment, and he added, "The boss there?"

"What is it?" Mary Ann had moved aside and Corny was hanging out of the window now.

"Had an American in a few minutes ago. Great big whopper of a car. . . . A Chevrolet. Twelve gallons of petrol and shots and oil, an' he gave me half-a-crown. Could do with some of those every hour, couldn't we, boss?"

"I'll say."

"He was tickled to death by me trombone, he laughed like a looney. He laughed all the time, even when I wasn't playing it. He must have thought I looked funny or summat, eh?"

"Well, as long as he gave you a tip, that's everything," said Corny. "I'll be down in a minute."

"O.K., boss."

After he had closed the window, Corny went straight into the

22

scullery and returned with a floor cloth with which he began to wipe the mess from the stove.

"Corny. Please. Leave it, I'll see to it."

Abruptly he stopped rubbing with the cloth, and without turning his head said, "I want to clean this up."

Standing back from him, Mary Ann looked at his ham-fisted actions with the cloth. There were depths in this husband of hers she couldn't fathom, there were facets of his thinking that she couldn't follow at times. There were things he did that wouldn't make sense to other people, like him wanting to clean up the mess his son had made. She said gently, "I'm going to wash them; will you come in?"

He went on rubbing for a moment. Then nodding towards the stove, he said, "I'll be in."

When he had the room to himself, and the egg and shell gathered on to the floor cloth, he stood with it in his hand looking down at it for a long moment. Life was odd, painful, and frightening at times.

2

Mary Ann liked Sundays. There were two kinds in her life, the winter Sundays and the summer Sundays. She didn't know which she liked best. Perhaps the winter Sundays, when Corny lay in bed until eight o'clock and she snuggled up in his arms and they talked about things they never got round to during the week. Then before the clock had finished striking eight, the twins would burst into the room—Rose Mary had her orders that they weren't to come in before eight o'clock on a Sunday, on a winter Sunday, because Dad liked a lie in.

On the summer Sundays, Corny rose at six and brought her a cup of tea before he went off to early Mass in Felling, and as soon as the door had closed on him the children would scamper into the bed and snuggle down, one each side of her, at least for a while. Eight o'clock on a summer Sunday morning usually found the bed turned into a rough house, and on such mornings Mary Ann became a girl again, a child, as she laughed and tumbled and giggled with her children. Sometimes she was up and had the breakfast ready for Corny's return, but more often she was struggling to bring herself back to the point of being a mother, with a mother's responsibility, when he returned.

But this summer Sunday morning Mary Ann was up and had Corny's breakfast ready on his return. Moreover, the children were dressed and both standing to the side of the breakfast table, straining their faces against the window-pane to catch a sight of the car coming along the road.

"He's a long time," Rose Mary commented, then added, "can I start on a piece of toast, Mam?"

"No, you can't. You'll wait till your dad comes in."

"I'm hungry, I could eat a horse. David's hungry an' all."

"Rose Mary!"

Rose Mary gave her shoulders a little shake, then turned from the window, and, moving the spoon that was set near her cereal bowl, she said, "I hope old Father Doughty doesn't take our Mass this mornin', 'cos he keeps on and on. He yammers."

"Rose Mary, you're not to talk like that."

"Well, Mam, he does."

"Well, if he does, it's for your own good. And you should listen and pay heed to what he says."

"I pay heed to Father Carey. I like Father Carey. Father Carey never frightens me."

Mary Ann turned from the sideboard and looked at her daughter; then asked quietly, "Are you frightened of Father Doughty?"

Rose Mary now took up her spoon and whirled it round her empty bowl before saying, "Sometimes. He was on about the Holy Ghost last Sunday and the sin of pride. Annabel Morton said he was gettin' at me 'cos I'm stuck up. I'm not stuck up, am I, Mam?"

"I should hope not. What have you to be stuck up about?"

"Well, it's because we've got a garage and it's me dad's."

"Oh." Mary Ann nodded and turned her head back to the cutlery drawer. "But I thought you said you weren't stuck up."

"Well, just a little bit. About me dad I am." The spoon whirled more quickly now. Then it stopped abruptly, and Rose Mary, turning to her mother, said, "What's the Holy Ghost like, Mam?"

"What?"

"I mean, what's he like? Is he like God? Or is he like Jesus?"

Mary Ann made a great play of separating the knives and forks in the drawer. Then, turning her head slightly towards her daughter but not looking at her, she said, "God and Jesus and the Holy Ghost are all the same, they all look alike."

"Oh no they don't."

Mary Ann's eyes were now brought sharply towards her daughter, to see a face that was almost a replica of her own, except for the eyes that were like Corny's, tilted pointedly upwards towards her. "Jesus is Jesus, and I know what Jesus looks

25

like 'cos I have pictures of him. An' I know who God looks like. But not the Holy Ghost."

Mary Ann's voice was very small when, looking down at her daughter, she said, "You know who God looks like? Who?"

"Me granda Shaughnessy. He's big like him, and nice and kind."

Mary Ann turned towards the drawer again before closing her eyes and putting her hand over her brow. Her da like God. Oh, she wanted to laugh. She wished Corny was here . . . he would have enjoyed that. Big, and nice, and kind. Well, and wasn't he all three? But for her da to take on the resemblance of God, Oh dear! Oh dear!"

"Aha!" The sound came from David who was still looking out of the window, and Rose Mary turned towards him, crying, "It's me dad."

Both the children now waved frantically out of the window, and Corny waved back to them.

The minute he entered the room they flew to him, and he lifted one up in each arm, to be admonished by Mary Ann, crying, "Now don't crush their clothes, they're all ready for Mass."

"Dad. Dad, who said seven o'clock?"

"Father Doughty."

"Oh, then Father Carey will say eight, and Father Doughty will say nine, and Father Carey will say ten. Oh goodie!" She flung her arms around his neck and pressed her face against his, and David, following suit, entwined his arms on top of hers and pressed his cheek against the other side of his father's face.

The business of Friday night was a thing of the past; it was Sunday and "family day".

Although the pattern of Sunday differed from winter to summer it had only been what Mary Ann thought of as "family day" since Jimmy had been taken on, because Jimmy came at eight o'clock on the summer Sunday mornings and stayed till ten, and, if required, he would come back again at two and stay as long as Corny wanted him. Jimmy was saving up for a motor-bike and Sunday work being time and a half he didn't mind how long he stayed. And when he was kept on on Sunday afternoon it meant they could all go to the farm together.

"Sit yourselves up," Mary Ann said, "and make a start. I'll take Jimmy's down."

Before she left the room they had all started on their cereal. When David had emptied his bowl he pushed it away from him, and Corny, looking down on his son, asked quietly, "Would you like some more, David?"

David looked brightly back into Corny's face and gave a small shake of his head, and Corny, putting his spoon gently down on to the table, took hold of his son's hand and said quietly, "Say . . . no . . . thank . . . you . . . Dad." He spaced the words.

David looked back at his father, and Rose Mary, her spoon poised halfway to her mouth, looked at David.

"Go on, say it," urged Corny, still softly. "No, thank you. Just say it. No . . . thank . . . you."

David's eyes darkened. The mischievous smile lurked in the back of them. He slanted his eyes now to Rose Mary, and Rose Mary, looking quickly at her father, said, "He wants to say no thank you, Dad. He means, no thank you, don't you, David?" She pushed her face close against his, and David smiled widely at her and nodded his head briskly, and Corny, picking up his spoon again, started eating.

Rose Mary stood with one hand in Mary Ann's while with the other she clutched at David's. She wasn't feeling very happy; it wasn't going to be a very nice Sunday. It hadn't been a very nice Sunday from the beginning, because her mother had got out of bed early, and then her dad had been vexed at breakfast time because David wouldn't say No thank you, and now they were going into Felling by bus.

Her mam had snapped at her when she asked her why her dad couldn't run them in in the car. She couldn't see why he couldn't close up the garage for a little while, just a little while, it didn't take long to get into Felling by car. And what was worse, worse for her mam anyway, was that she had to go all the way to Jarrow by bus. She didn't like it when her mam went to Jarrow Church, but she only went to Jarrow Church when she was visiting Greatgran McBride, killing two birds with one stone, she called it. She herself liked to visit Greatgran

McBride, and so did David. They loved going to Greatgran McBride's. They didn't mind the smell.

"Mam, couldn't you leave going to Greatgran McBride's until this afternoon?"

"Don't you want to go to the farm this afternoon?"

"Yes, but I'd like to go to Greatgran McBride's an' all. Dad could run us there afore we went to the farm."

"Dad can't do any such thing, so stop it. And don't you start on that when we get home. I'm going to see Greatgran McBride because she isn't well and she can't be bothered with children around."

"She always says she loves to——" .

"You're not going to-day."

There was a short silence before Rose Mary suggested, "Couldn't we come on after Mass? We could meet you an' we could all come back together. I could get the bus; I've done it afore."

"Do you want me to get annoyed with you, Rose Mary?"

"No, Mam." The voice was very small.

"Well, then, do as you're told. What's the matter with you this morning?"

"I think it might be Father Doughty an' I don't like——"

"You know it'll be Father Carey. And not another word now, here's the bus, and behave yourself."

Twenty minutes later, Rose Mary, still holding David by the hand, entered St. Patrick's Church. Inside the doorway she reached up and dipped her fingers in the holy-water font, and David followed suit; then one after the other they genuflected to the main altar. This done, they walked down the aisle until they came to the fifth pew from the front. This was one of the pews allotted to their class. Again they genuflected one after the other, then Rose Mary entered the pew first. One foot on the wooden kneeler, one on the floor, she was making her way to where sat her school pals, Jane Leonard and Katie Eastman, when she became aware that she was alone, at least, in-as-much as the other half of her was not immediately behind her. She turned swiftly, to see David standing in the aisle looking up at Miss Plum. Miss Plum had David by one hand and David was hanging on to the end of the pew with the other. Swiftly, Rose Mary made the return journey to the aisle, and Miss Plum, bending down to her and answering her look, which said plainly, "Now what are you up to with our David?" whispered, "I'm putting David with the boys on the other side."

"But, Miss Plum, he won't go."

A low hissing whisper now from Miss Plum. "He'll go if you tell him to, Rose Mary."

A whisper now from Rose Mary. "But I've told him afore, Miss Plum."

"Go and sit down, Rose Mary, and leave David to me."

Rose Mary stared up into Miss Plum's face. Then she looked at David, and David looked at her. Whereupon David, after a moment, turned his gaze towards Miss Plum again and made a sound that was much too loud for church. The sound might have been interpreted as, "Gert yer!" But, of course, David never said any such thing. He just made a sound of protest, but it was enough to put Miss Plum into action. In one swift movement she unloosened his fingers from the end of the pew and, inserting both her hands under his armpits, she whisked him across the aisle, plonked him none too gently on the wooden pew, then sat down beside him.

David made no more protesting sounds. He gazed up at the straight profile of his teacher, stared at her for a moment with his mouth open, then bent forward, to see beyond her waist, to find out what Rose Mary was up to in all this. He was now further surprised to see his sister, miles away from him, kneeling, with her chin on the pew rail staring towards the high altar. His brows gathered, the corners of his eyes puckered up. He was very puzzled. Rose Mary wasn't doing anything. He gave a wriggle with his bottom to bring him further forward, when a hand, that almost covered the whole of his chest, pushed him backwards on the seat, making him over-balance and bump his head and bring his legs abruptly up to his eye level.

When Rose Mary, from the corner of her eye, saw Miss Plum push their David and knock his head against the pew, she almost jumped up and shouted out loud, but, being in church, she had to restrain her actions and content herself with her thoughts.

She hated Miss Plum, she did, she did. And David wouldn't know anything about the Mass. He wouldn't understand what Frather Carey was saying, and he wouldn't be able to sing the hymn inside hisself like he did when he was with her. . . . Wait till she got home, she would tell her dad about Miss Plum. Just wait. She would get him to come to the school the morrow and let her have it. Plum, Plum, Plum. She hoped a big plum stone would stick in her gullet and she would die. She did, she did. In the name of the Father, and of the Son, and of the Holy Ghost. Amen.

. Father Carey was kneeling on the altar steps. "Our Father Who art in heaven, hallowed be Thy name." She had taken their David across there all because of Annabel Morton, 'cos last Sunday when Annabel Morton had punched their David under her coat so nobody could see, David had kicked her and made her shout out. . . . "An' forgive us our trespasses, as we forgive them that trespass against us." Miss Plum had blamed her and she wouldn't believe about Annabel Morton punching David and she had been nasty all the week. Oh, she did hate Miss Plum. Their poor David havin' to sit there all by hisself, all through the Mass, and it would go on for hours and hours. Father Carey was talking slow, he was taking his time, he always did. "I believe in God the Father Almighty, Creator of Heaven and Earth." If her dad wouldn't come down and go for Miss Plum the morrow she knew who would. Her Grandad Shaughnessy would. He would soon tell her where she got off. Yes, that's who would give it to her, her Grandad Shaughnessy. "I believe in the Holy Ghost, the Holy Catholic Church." And Father Carey would likely go on about the Holy Ghost and the Trinity this morning; when he started his sermon he forgot to stop, although he made you laugh at times. Oh, she wished the Mass was over. She slanted her eyes to the left, but she couldn't see anything, only the bowed heads of the other three girls who were filling up the pew now. If she raised her chin and stuck it on the arm rest she had a view of Miss Plum, but there was no sign of David. Poor David was somewhere down on the kneeler yon side of Miss Plum. Well, it would serve Miss Plum right if he started to scream.

Rose Mary brought her head slowly forward and she looked to where the priest was mounting the steps towards the altar. But she wasn't interested at all in what Father Carey was doing, for forming a big question mark in her mind was the word WHY? . . . WHY? . . . Why hadn't he screamed? Why wasn't their David screaming? He always screamed when he was separated from her? Perhaps Miss Plum was holding his mouth. She jerked round so quickly in the direction of her teacher that she overbalanced and fell across the calves of the girl next to her.

When a hand came down and righted her more quickly than she had fallen, she caught a fleeting glimpse of its owner, and now, staring wide-eyed towards the altar again, she wondered how on earth Miss Watson had got behind her. Miss Watson was the headmistress. Miss Watson usually sat at the back of the church in solitary state.

As the Mass went on the awful thought of Miss Watson behind her kept Rose Mary's gaze fixed on the altar, except when she was getting on or off her seat to stand or kneel, when her head would accidentally turn to the left. But she might as well have kept it straight, for all she could see past the bodies of her schoolmates was the tall, full figure of Miss Plum. No sight, and what was more puzzling still, no sound of their David. . . .

The Mass over at last, Rose Mary came out of the pew in line with the others, genuflected deeply, then looked towards Miss Plum. But Miss Plum's profile was cast in marble, in fact her whole body seemed stone-like. A push from behind and Rose Mary was forced to go up the aisle, and she daren't look round, for there at the top stood Miss Watson. She bowed her head as she passed Miss Watson as if she, too, demanded adoration.

Outside, she waited, her eyes glued on the church door. All the girls had come out first, and now came the boys . . . but not their David, and not Miss Plum. The grown-ups appeared in a long straggling line, and among them was Miss Watson, but still no sign of Miss Plum. Rose Mary could stand it no longer. Sidling back into the church, she looked down the aisle, and there, standing next to Miss Plum and opposite Father Carey, was their David, looking as if nothing had happened. The priest was smiling, and Miss Plum was smiling, and they were talking in whispers. When they turned, David turned, and they all came up the aisle towards her. And when they reached her Miss Plum looked down on her and said, "David's been a very good boy, and he's going to sit with me every Sunday."

Rose Mary sent a sweeping glance from Miss Plum to David, then from David to Father Carey, and back to Miss Plum. She was opening her mouth to protest when the priest said, "Isn't that a great favour, David, eh?" He had his hand on David's head. "Sitting next to your teacher. My My. Everybody else in the class will be jealous." He now looked at Miss Plum, and Miss Plum at him, and they smiled at each other. And then Miss Plum said, "Good-bye, Father." She said it like Annabel Morton said things when she was sucking up to somebody. Then she went out of the church.

Rose Mary, now grasping David's hand, looked at the priest, and said softly, "Father."

"Yes, Rose Mary." He bent his head towards her.

"Father, our David doesn't like being by hisself."

"But he hasn't been by his—himself, he's been sitting next to Miss Plum, and liked it."

"He doesn't like it, Father."

"Now, now, Rose Mary. David's getting a big boy and he must sit with the big boys, musn't you, David?" The young priest turned towards David, and David grinned at him.

Rose Mary contemplated the priest. She liked Father Carey, she did, he was lovely, but he just didn't understand the situation. She now jerked her chin up towards him, and whispered, "Father." The word was in the form of a request that he should lend her his ear, and this he did, literally putting it near her mouth, and what he heard was, "He can't talk without me, Father."

Now it was Rose Mary's turn to lend him her ear and into it he whispered, "But he doesn't talk now, Rose Mary."

Now the exchange was made again, and what he heard this time was, "He does to me, Father."

Again a movement of heads and a whisper, "But we want him to talk to everybody, don't we, Rose Mary?"

"Yes, Father . . . oh, yes, Father. But . . ."

The priest whisked his ear away, straightened up and said, "We'll have to pray to our Lady about it."

"But I have, Father, an' she hasn't done anything. . . . Perhaps if you asked her, Father."

"Yes, yes, I'll ask her." Father Carey drew his fingers down his nose.

"When?" She could talk now quite openly because their David didn't know what it was all about.

"Oh, at Mass in the morning."

"The first Mass, Father?"

Father Carey's eyebrows moved slightly upwards and he hesitated slightly before saying, "Yes. Yes, the first Mass."

"Could you make it the half-past eight one, Father?"

The priest's eyebrows rose farther; then his head dropped forward as if he was tired, and he looked at Rose Mary for a moment before saying slowly, "Well, if you would like it that way, all right. Yes, I'll do it at the second Mass."

"Thank you, Father." She bestowed on him her nice smile, the one that had earned the unwarranted title of angelic, then she finished: "An' now we'd better get home, 'cos me mam worries if we're late. We'll have to run, I think."

"That's it, run along. Good-bye, David." The priest patted David's head. "Good-bye, Rose Mary." He chucked her under the chin; then with a hand on each of them he pressed them towards the church door, and then for a moment he watched them running down the street, and he shook his head as he thought, Dear, dear. It was as Miss Plum said, she had her work cut out with that little lady. It was also true that the boy would make little progress as long as he had a mouthpiece in his sister. And what a mouthpiece, she'd talk the hind leg off a donkey. He re-entered the church, laughing.

Rose Mary walked down the street and away from the church in silence, and the unusualness of this procedure caused David to trip over his feet as he gazed at his sister instead of looking where he was going. Then of a sudden, he was pulled to a stop, and Rose Mary, bending towards him, said under her breath, "Father Carey's going to tell Our Lady to ask God to make you

33

speak the morrow mornin', he's goin' to tell her at the half-past eight. And you will, won't you, David?"

David's eyes darkened, and shone, his smile widened and he nodded his head once.

Rose Mary sighed. Then she, too, smiled. That was that then. Everything was taken care of. If things went right he should be talking just when they reached their classroom.

Getting on the bus, Rose Mary reminded David, in no small voice now, that it being Sunday they'd have Yorkshire pudding and if he liked he could have his with milk and sugar before his dinner; then she went on to explain what there would be for the dinner, not forgetting to pay stress on the delectability of the pudding. Following this she gave him a description of what there was likely to be for tea at Gran Shaughnessy's. By the time they alighted from the bus the other occupants had no doubt in their minds but that Rose Mary and David Boyle had a mother who was a wonderful cook, a father who could supply unstintingly the necessities to further his wife's art, and grandparents who apparently lived like lords. And this was as it should be, otherwise she would have indeed wasted her breath.

3

Lizzie Shaughnessy looked at her daughter from under her lowered lids. When they were alone like this it was always hard to believe that her Mary Ann was a married woman and the mother of twins, for she still looked so young and childlike herself. It was her small stature that tended towards this impression, she thought.

Lizzie knew that her daughter was worried and she was waiting for her to unburden herself, and she knew the substance of her worry: it was the child. She joined on another ounce of wool to her knitting, then said, "Do you know what they're going to do with Peter?"

"Send him to boarding school," Mary Ann said.

Lizzie slowly put her knitting on to her lap and, turning her head right round to Mary Ann, said, "Who told you?"

"Nobody, but I guesed it would come. I remember years ago Tony saying that Mr. Lord had a school all mapped out for the boy."

"But neither Tony nor Lettice wants to send him away to school."

"I know that, but he'll go all the same; they'll send him because that's what Mr. Lord wants. He always gets what he wants."

"Not always," said Lizzie quietly. And to this Mary Ann made no rejoinder, for she knew that one of the great disappointments in her mother's life, and Mr. Lord's, was when his grandson and herself hadn't made a match of it.

"The old man will be the one who will miss him most," Lizzie went on. "But it amazes me that he can put up with the boy; he's so noisy and boisterous and he never stops talking. . . ."

Mary Ann got up from her chair and walked to the sitting-room window, and Lizzie said softly, "I'm sorry, I wasn't meaning to make comparisons. You know that, oh you know that."

"Of course I do, Ma." Mary Ann looked at her mother over her shoulder. "It's all right. Don't be silly; I didn't take it to myself, it's just that . . ." She spread out her hands, and then came back to her seat and sat down before ending, "I just can't understand it. He's not deaf, he's certainly not dim, and yet he can't talk."

"He will. Be patient, he will. . . . You . . . you wouldn't consider leaving him with us?"

"Corny's been at you, hasn't he?"

"No. No." Lizzie shook her head vigorously.

"Oh, don't tell me, Ma. I bet my bottom dollar he has. He thinks that if they were separated, even for a short time, it would make David talk. It wouldn't. And Rose Mary wouldn't be able to bear it. Neither would David, they're inseparable. At any rate, the doctor himself said it wouldn't be any use separating them."

"You could give it a trial." Lizzie had her eyes fixed on her knitting now.

"No, Ma, no. I wouldn't have one worry then, I'd have two, for I just don't know what the effect would be on Rose Mary, because she just lives and breathes for that boy."

"Yes, that's your trouble." Lizzie was now looking straight at her daughter. "That's the trouble, she lives and breathes for him."

"Oh, Ma, don't you start."

"All right, all right. We'll say no more. Anyway, here they come. . . . And don't look like that else they'll know something has happened. Come on, cheer up." She rose from her seat and put her hand on Mary Ann's shoulder, adding under her breath, "It'll be all right; it'll come out all right, you'll see."

"Gran, Gran, Peter's got new riding breeches. Look!" Rose Mary dashed into the room, followed by a dark-haired, dark-eyed, pale-faced boy of seven.

"Have you all wiped your feet?" was Lizzie's greeting to them.

"Yes, Granma," cried Rose Mary. "An' David has, an' all."

"An' I have too, Granshan."

36

This quaint combination of the beginning of her name with the courtesy title of Gran attached had been given to her by Tony's son from the time he could talk. To him she had become Granshan, and now it was an accepted title and no one laughed at it any more.

Following Peter, Sarah hobbled into the room. She was still on sticks, still crippled with polio as she would be all her days, but moving more agilely than she had done nearly seven years ago, when she had stood for the first time since her illness at the altar to be married. Behind her came Michael, refraining, as always, from helping her except by his love, which still seemed to hallow them both, and behind Michael, and looking just an older edition of him, came Mike.

Mike's red hair was now liberally streaked with grey. He had put on a little more weight, but he still looked a fine strapping figure of a man, and the hook, which for a long time had been a substitute for his left hand, was now replaced by thin steel fingers that seemed to move of their own volition.

Mike, now turning a laughing face over his shoulder, asked of Corny who was in the hall, "You wiped your feet?"

"No," said Corny, coming to the room door. "I never wipe my feet; it's a stand I've made against all house-proud women, never to wipe my feet."

"You know better," said Lizzie, nodding across the room at him. Then she cried at the throng about her, "I don't know what you all want in here when the tea's laid and you should be sitting down."

"Am I to stay to tea, Granshan?"

Lizzie looked down on the boy and said, "Of course, Peter, but you'd better tell your mother, hadn't you?"

"Oh, she knows." He wagged his head at her. "I told her you'd likely invite me."

In his disarming way he joined in the roar that followed, and when Michael cuffed him playfully on the head the boy turned on him with doubled-up fists, and there ensued a sparring match, which David and Rose Mary applauded, jumping and shouting around them. It was the fact of David shouting that brought Corny's and Mary Ann's hands together, because the boy was

37

actually making an intelligible sound which could almost be interpreted as "Go on, Peter. Go on, Peter."

Mary Ann's head drooped slightly and she made a small groaning sound as her mother's voice brought the sparring to an end with a sharp command of, "Now give over. Do you hear me, Michael, stop it. If you want any rough-house stuff, get you outside, the lot of you. Come on now."

Michael collapsed on the couch, and this was the signal for the three children to storm over him, and Lizzie, turning to the rest, commanded, "Get yourselves into the other room and seated . . . I'll see to these."

Five minutes later they were all seated round the well-laden tea table. There had been a little confusion over the seating in the first place as Rose Mary wanted to sit next to Peter, and Peter evidently wanted to sit next to Rose Mary, but David not only wanted to sit next to Rose Mary, he also wanted to sit next to Peter, so in the end David sat between Peter and Rose Mary and the tea got under way.

It was in the middle of tea, when Corny and Mary Ann between them were giving their version of Jimmy's trombone playing, that Peter suddenly said, "I'd jolly well like to hear him. They've got a band at school, but it's just whistles and things. Perhaps Father will bring me over to-morrow when he comes to see you, and I'll hear him play then, eh, Uncle Corny?"

"Tony . . . your father's coming to see me to-morrow, Peter?" Corny looked down the table towards the boy, and Peter, his head cocked on one side, said, "Yes, he said he was. He wants a new car, and you're going to buy it for him."

"Oh?"

All eyes were on Corny. This was a good bit of news, it meant business, yet the elders at the table knew that Corny wasn't taking it like that. To get an order from Tony, who was the grandson of Mr. Lord, Mr. Lord who had for so long been Mary Ann's mentor and who was still finding ways and means of handing out help to her, would not meet with Corny's approval, even if it meant badly needed business.

Mike's voice broke the immediate silence at the table, saying, "You've spilt the beans, young fellow, haven't you?"

38

Peter looked towards the man, whom, in his own mind, he considered one of his family, and said, with something less than his usual exuberance, "Yes, Granpa Shan, I have . . . Father will be vexed." He now turned his gaze down the table towards Corny and said, "I'm sorry, Uncle Corny. I wasn't supposed to know, I just overheard Father telling Mother . . . I'll get it in the neck now, I suppose." The last statement, said in such a polite tone, was too much even for Corny. He laughed, and the tension was broken as he said, "And you deserve to get it in the neck too, me lad."

"You won't give me away to Father?" Peter was leaning over his plate as he looked down towards Corny, and Corny, narrowing his eyes at the young culprit, said, "What's it worth?"

This remark brought Peter upright. He looked first towards Rose Mary's bright face, then towards David's penetrating stare, and, his agile mind working overtime, he returned his gaze to Corny and said, "Let's say I'll help to clean one of your cars for you during the holidays . . . that's if I can stay to dinner."

They were all laughing and all talking at once, and Sarah, leaning across the corner of the table towards Mary Ann, said, "He'll either grow up to be Foreign Minister, or a confidence trickster," whereupon they both laughed louder still.

But behind her laughter a little nagging voice was saying to Mary Ann: If only David had said that; and he could have, he could be as cute as Peter any day, if only he could break through the skin that was covering his speech.

If only. If only. If only there was some way. . . . But not separating them as Corny wanted, and now her mother. No, not that way.

4

It was half-past ten in the morning and a beautiful day; cars were spinning thick and fast over all the roads in England, and the North had more than its share of traffic. There were people going on their holidays to the Lake District, to Scotland, to Wales. There were foreigners in cars who were discovering that the North of England had more to show than pits and docks. Yet Corny, who had been in the garage since half-past six that morning, had sold exactly four gallons of petrol.

It couldn't go on, he had just told himself as he sat in his little office looking at his ledger. Last week he had cleared seventeen pounds, and he'd had Jimmy to pay out of that, and then there had been the building society repayments, insurance, and the usual sum to be put by for rates, and what did that leave for living? They had dipped into their savings so often, the money they had banked from Mr. Lord's generous wedding present to them both, until it was now very near the bottom of the barrel. Mary Ann worked miracles, but at times there was a fear in him that she would get tired of working miracles. She was young, they were both young, and they weren't seeing much of life, only hard work and struggling. This was what both his parents and hers had had in their young days, but the young of to-day were supposed to be having it easy, making so much money in fact that they didn't know what to do with it, or themselves. And it was a fact in some cases. There was his brother, Dan, twenty-four years old, not a thought in his head but beer and women, and yet he never picked up less than thirty quid from his lorry driving; forty-five quid some weeks he had told him, and just for dumping clay, not even stepping a foot out of his cab.

Life at this moment appeared very unfair. Why, Corny asked

40

himself, couldn't he get a break? Nobody worked harder, tried harder. It was funny how your life could be altered by one man's vote in a committee room. When he had bought the garage seven years ago he had been sure that the council would widen the lane and make it into a main connecting road between Felling and Turnstile point, but one man's vote had potched the whole thing. . . . But not quite. It was the "not quite" that had kept him hanging on, for there had been rumours that the council had ideas for this little bottle-neck. Some said they were going to buy the land near the old turnstile for a building estate. Another rumour was that they were going to build a comprehensive school just across the road in what was known as Weaver's field.

During the first couple of years he had sustained himself on the rumours. He seemed to have been very young then, even gullible, now he knew he was no longer young inside, and certainly not gullible. No rumour affected him any more; yet at the same time he kept hanging on, and hoping.

He rose from the stool and walked out into the bright sunshine. Everything looked neat and tidy. Nobody, he assured himself, had a prettier garage. The red flowers against the white stones, the cement drive-in all scrubbed clean, not a spot of oil to be seen—perhaps that was a bad sign, he should leave the oily patches, it would bear out the old saying: where there was dirt there was money. He turned and looked into the big garage. It, too, was too tidy, too bare. He hadn't a thing in for repairs. The garage held nothing now but his old Rover and some cardboard adverts for tyres.

As he stared down the long, empty space Jimmy came from out of the shadows with a broom in his hand, and, leaning on it and looking towards Corny, he said quizzically, "Well, that's that. What next, boss? . . . There's a bird's nest in the chimney, I could go and tidy that up. . . ."

"Now I'm having none of that . . . an' you mind." Corny's voice came as a growl, and Jimmy, the smile sliding from his face, said, "I was only kiddin', boss. I meant nowt, honest."

"Well, let's hope you didn't. I've told you afore, if you don't like it here there's plenty of other jobs you can get. I'm not stopping you. You knew the terms when you started."

"Aye. Aye, I know. An' it's all right with me. I like it here, I've told you, 'cos I've learned more with you than I would have done in a big garage, stuck on one job. . . . It's only, well. . . ." Jimmy didn't go on to explain that he got bored when there were no jobs in but said, with a touch of excitement, "Look, what about me takin' that monstrosity out there to bits and buryin' it, eh?"

He walked past Corny, and Corny slowly followed him to the edge of the garage, and they looked towards his piece of spare land that bordered the garden and where stood a car. Three nights ago someone had driven a car there and left it. The first indication Corny had of this was when he opened up the next morning, and the sight of the dumped car almost brought his temper to boiling point. They just wanted to start that; let that get round and before he knew where he was he'd be swamped. They had started that game up near the cemetery, and there were two graveyards up there now. He couldn't understand how he'd slept through someone driving a car down the side of the building, because a car had only to pass down the road in the night and it would wake him, and he would say to himself, "It couldn't come down in the daytime, could it."

He had been on the point of taking a hammer and doing what Jimmy suggested they should do now, break the thing up and bury it, but the twins had caused him to change his mind, at least temporarily, for Rose Mary had begged him to let them have it to play with, and strangely, Mary Ann had backed her up, saying, "It would give them something to do now that they were on holiday, and might stop her pestering to be taken to the sands at Whitley Bay or Shields. So Corny had been persuaded against his will to leave the car as it was. He had siphoned out what petrol there remained in the tank, cleared the water and oil out, and left the children with a gigantic toy, hoping that their interest might lag within a few days and he would then dispose of it. But the few days had passed and their interest, far from waning, had increased.

From where he stood he could see the pair of them, Rose Mary in the driving seat with David bobbing up and down beside her, driving to far-off places he had no doubt, places as far away as their Greatgran McBride's in Jarrow. He smiled quietly to himself as he thought they were like him in that way, he had always wanted to go to his Grannie McBride, for his grannie's cluttered untidy house had been more of home to him than his real home; and it had been her dominant, loud, yet wise personality that had kept him steady. . . . Yes, undoubtedly, the pair of them would be off in the car to their Greatgran McBride's.

"No go, boss?"

Corny gave a huh! of a laugh as he turned to Jimmy and said, "What do you think? Go down there and tell them you're going to smash it up and there'll be blue murder."

"Well, what'll I do?" Jimmy was looking straight up into Corny's face, and Corny surveyed him for a full minute before answering, "Well now, what would you like to do?"

On this question the corner of Jimmy's mouth was drawn in, and he looked downwards at his feet as if considering. Then, his eyes flicking upwards again, he glanced at Corny and they both laughed.

"Well, mind, just until the missus comes in. I'll give you the tip when I see her coming up the road, for she's threatened to leave me if she hears any more of your efforts."

Jimmy's mouth split his face, and on a loud laugh, he said, "Aw! I can see her doing that, boss. But ta, I'll stop the minute you give me the nod."

Less than a minute later the too quiet air of the garage and the immediate vicinity was broken by the anguished, hesitant wails of the trombone.

The sound had no effect on Corny one way or the other. He had practised his cornet so much as a lad that he now seemed immune to the awful wailing wind practice evoked. Although when he stopped to think about it the boy was learning, and fast, in spite of the quivering screeches and wrong notes.

He was in the office again when he heard a car approaching the garage and almost instantly he was outside, rubbing his hands with a cloth as if he had just come off a grimy job. The car might pass, yet again it might stop. He had noticed before that the sight of someone about the place induced people to stop, but

43

apparently this car needed no inducement, for it swirled on to the drive and braked almost at his feet.

Jimmy's American.

Corny recognized the Chevrolet and the driver, inasmuch as the latter's nationality was indicated by his dress, particularly his hat.

"Hello, there." The man was getting out of the car.

"Good morning, sir."

The man was tall, as tall as Corny himself, and broad with it. Like most Americans, he looked well dressed and, as Corny thought, finished off. He was a man who could have been forty, or fifty, there was no telling. He was clean-shaven, with deep brown eyes and a straight-lipped mouth. His face had an all-over pleasantness, and his manner was decidedly so. Without moving his feet he leaned his body back and looked up through the empty garage, and, his face slipping into a wide grin, he said, "The youngster's at it again?"

"Oh yes. He's gone on the trombone. I let him have a go at it. . . ." He just stopped himself from adding "when we're not busy". Instead he said, "They're forming a new group and he's mad to learn."

"He's not your boy?"

"Oh no. No." Corny turned his head to one side, but his eyes still held those of the American. "Give us a chance."

"Of course, of course." The American's hand came out and pushed him familiarly in the shoulder. "You in your middle twenties I should say, and him nearing his twenties." His laugh was deep now. "You would have to have started early."

"You're saying!"

"Well now." He looked towards his car. "I want it filled, and do you think you could give her a wash?"

"Certainly, sir."

"Not very busy this morning?"

"No, not yet; it's early in the day. A lot of my customers work on a Saturday morning, you know, and they . . . they bring them in later."

"Yes, yes."

As Corny filled the tank with petrol the American walked to

44

one end of the building, then to the other. He stood looking for a moment at the children climbing over the car. Then coming back, he walked into the empty garage, and when he came out again he stood at Corny's side and said, "Happen you don't have a car for hire, do you?"

"No. No, sir. I'm sorry, I don't run hire cars."

"It's a pity. I wanted this one looked over, I've been running her hard for weeks and I've got the idea she's blown a gasket. I'm staying in Newcastle, but I want a car to get me back and forwards until this one is put right. . . . You've a car of your own, of course?"

"Only the old Rover, sir."

"Oh, that one in there? She looks in spanking condition." He walked away from Corny again and into the garage, and Corny, getting the hose to wash the Chevrolet down, thought, "That's what I want, a car for hire. I've said it afore. Look what I'm losing now, and it isn't the first time."

"Do you mind if I try her?"

"What's that, sir?" Corny went to the opening of the garage. The American had the Rover's door open and was bending forward examining her inside, and, straightening up, he called again, "Do you mind if I try her?"

"Not in the least, sir. But she's an old car and everything will be different."

The American had his back bent again, and he swung his head round to Corny and his mouth twisted as he said, "I was in England during the war, and after, I bet I've driven her mother."

They exchanged smiles, and then the American seated himself behind the wheel. "Can I take her along the road?"

"Do as you like, sir." Corny stood aside and looked at the man in the car as he handled the gear lever and moved his feet, getting the feel of her.

"O.K.?" He nodded towards Corny, and Corny nodded back to him, saying, "O.K., sir," and the next minute Fanny, as Mary Ann had christened the car after Mrs. McBride, moved quietly out of the garage, and Corny watched the back of her disappearing down the road.

He would have to take her right to the end before he turned, he thought, but that bloke knew what he was doing, he was driving her as if along a white line. She looked good from the back, as she did from the front, dignified, solid. He wasn't ashamed of Fanny, not for himself he wasn't.

Well, he'd better get on cleaning this one down. He was a nice chap was the American. No big talk. Well, not as yet, but you could usually tell from the start. . . . Lord, this was a car . . . and look at the boot, nearly as big as a Mini.

He had almost finished hosing the car down before the American returned. He brought the Rover on to the drive and, getting out, came towards Corny and said, "You wouldn't think of letting her out for a day or two?"

"The Rover? To you?" Corny's mouth was slightly agape.

"Yes, she's a fine old girl. You wouldn't mind?"

"Mind? Why should I mind, when you are leaving this one?" He thumbed toward the Chevrolet.

"Yes, I see what you mean, but, you know, I consider that many a wreck of a Rover is a sight more reliable than some of the new models that are going about now."

"You're right there, sir; you're right there."

"Well then, if you would hire her to me you could go over this one." He pointed towards his car.

"If it suits you, sir, it suits me."

"That's settled then."

An extra loud wail from Jimmy's trombone reverberated round the garage at this moment. It went high and shrill, then on a succession of stumbling notes fell away and left the American with his head back, his mouth wide open, and laughing heartily, very like, Corny thought, Mike laughed.

"You know." He began to dry his eyes. "I've thought a lot about that young chappie since I saw him last, and I always couple his face with the trombone. . . . No offence meant. It's a kind of face that goes with a trombone, don't you think, long an' lugubrious."

"Yes, I suppose so, looking at it like that." Corny, too, was laughing.

"Will you stop that noise, Jimmy!"

The voice not only hit Jimmy, but startled the two men, and they turned and looked to where Mary Ann was standing at the far end of the garage. She had come in by the back door and the children were with her.

"Coo, Mrs. Boyle, I thought you was out."

"Which means I suppose that every time I leave the house you play that thing. Now I'm warning you, Jimmy, if I hear it again I'll take it from you and I'll put a hammer to it. . . . Mind, I mean it."

"Aw, Mrs. Boyle. . . ."

Mary Ann turned hastily away, taking the children with her, and Jimmy came slowly down the garage, the trombone dangling from his hand. The American began to chuckle. Then, looking at Corny, he said softly, "That was Mrs. Boyle?"

"You're right; that was Mrs. Boyle," said Corny, below his breath.

The American shook his head. "She looks like a young girl, a young teenager, no more. But there's one thing sure; no matter what she looks like, she acts like a woman."

"And you're right there, too, sir." Corny jerked his head at the American. "She acts like a woman all right, and all the time."

The American laughed again; then said, "Well now, about you letting me have your old girl. Oh, make no mistake about it, I'm referring to the car." His head went back and again he was laughing, and Corny with him, while Jimmy·stood looking at them both from inside the garage.

"It's up to you, sir."

"All right, it's up to me, and I'll settle for a charge when I pick up my car. You won't be out of pocket, don't you worry. You won't know at this stage how long it's going to take you to do her, but I'll look in to-morrow, eh?"

"Do that, sir. If there's nothing very serious I should have her ready by then."

"Oh, there's no hurry. I'll enjoy driving the old lady."

"Corny."

The American now looked over Corny's shoulder to where a petite young girl—this was how he saw Mary Ann—was standing

47

at the door of the house. Corny, following the American's gaze, turned to see Mary Ann, and Mary Ann, her head drooping slightly, said quickly, "Oh, I'm sorry, I didn't know you were busy. I just came to tell you. . . ." Her voice trailed off.

The American was smiling towards Mary Ann, and Corny, motioning towards her with his hand, said, "This is my wife, sir." Whereupon, with characteristic friendliness, the American held out his hand as he walked towards her, saying, "The name's Blenkinsop."

"How do you do, Mr. Blenkinsop." Mary Ann smiled up at the American and liked what she saw. And now Corny said, "Mr. Blenkinsop's taking our car for a day or so while I do his."

"Our c . . . car?" Her mouth opened wide and she looked towards the Chevrolet. Then she turned her gaze towards Corny, and he said, "Mr. Blenkinsop knows she's an oldun but he's driven Rovers before."

"Oh." Mary Ann gave a small smile, but she still couldn't see how a man who drove this great chrome and cream machine could even bear to get into their old Rover.

At this moment Rose Mary and David put in an appearance. They came tearing out of the garage, and when they reached Mary Ann, Rose Mary didn't take in the presence of the American for a moment before she said, "You wouldn't break up Jimmy's trombone, would you, Mam? I told him you were only funnin'."

Mary Ann looked at the American; she looked at Corny; then, shaking her head, she looked at her daughter and said, "I'm not funning, and you go back and tell Jimmy that I'm not funning."

There was a pause before she added, "He's practising the trombone and he makes a dreadful racket." She was addressing the American now, and she was surprised when he let out a deep rumbling laugh as he said, "I know." Then, the smile slipping from his face, he asked her in all seriousness, "You don't think he's funny?"

"Funny! Making that noise?" Mary Ann screwed up her face. "No, I don't."

"Well! Well! Well! It just goes to show. You know, Mrs. Boyle, he's the only thing that's given me a belly laugh since I

48

came to England. Plays, musical comedies, the lot, I've seen them all and I've never had a good laugh until I saw that boy's face as he sat blowing that trombone. As I was just saying to your husband, he's got a face for the trombone."

Mary Ann smiled. She smiled with her mouth closed, and she looked at Corny as she did so. Then looking back at the American, she said, "The difference is, you don't have to live above the racket."

"I wouldn't mind."

"You wouldn't?"

"No."

"Well, there's a pair of you." She nodded to Corny. "He doesn't mind it at all, but I really can't stand it, it gets on my nerves."

The American now lowered his head and moved it from side to side, looking at Corny as he remarked, "It's as I said, she acts like a woman. They're unpredictable." He turned his head now towards Mary Ann and smiled broadly, then added, "Well now, I must be off. I've got a lunch appointment for one o'clock. . . . Here." He beckoned to the children. Then, putting his hand in his pocket and pulling out his wallet, he flicked a pound note from a bundle and handed it to Rose Mary, saying, "Split that between you and get some pop and candy."

"Oh, thank you."

Before Rose Mary had finished speaking, Mary Ann said, "Oh, sir, no; that's too much." She took the note from Rose Mary, whose fingers were reluctant to release it, and she handed it back to Mr. Blenkinsop, and he, his face looking blank, now asked rather sharply, "What's the matter? Don't they have ice creams or candies or such?"

"Yes, yes, but this is too——"

"Nonsense." His tone was sharp, and he turned abruptly from her and, speaking to Corny in the same manner, he said, "Well, I'll be off. See you to-morrow."

Mr. Blenkinsop got in the Rover and started her up; then, leaning out of the window, he said, "How's she off for petrol?"

"She's full."

"That's good. See you."

"Yes. See you, sir." Corny smiled at Mr. Blenkinsop, then raised his hand and stood watching the car going down the road before turning to Mary Ann.

Mary Ann, with the pound note still in her hand, held it towards him, saying, "He must be rolling, and he must be bats or a bit eccentric to go off in ours."

"What do you mean, bats or a bit eccentric, there's nothing wrong with our car?"

"No, I'm not saying there is, but you know what I mean. Look at it compared with that." She pointed to the Chevrolet.

"You're just going by externals. Let me tell you that the engine in the Rover will still be going when this one's on the scrap heap."

"Yes, yes, I suppose so, but it's the looks of the thing. Anyway," she sighed, "he seems a nice enough man."

"Nice enough?" said Corny, walking towards the car. "He's a godsend."

"I wonder what he's doing round these parts," said Mary Ann.

"I don't know," said Corny, "but I hope he stays."

"Can we keep it, Mam?"

"What?" Mary Ann looked down at her daughter, then said, "Oh yes. Yes, you may, but you're not going to spend it all, either of you. You can have half-a-crown each, and the rest goes in your boxes."

"Oh, splash!" said Rose Mary. "I know what I'm going to buy. Can we go into Felling this afternoon, Mam?"

"I suppose so." Mary Ann turned abruptly towards Corny, saying, "By the way, what did he mean, I act like a woman?"

Corny brought his head from under the bonnet of the car and, laughing towards her, said, "He took you for a young girl, a real young girl, and then when he heard you going for Jimmy he said you acted like a woman."

"Well, I should hope I do act like a woman. What did he expect me to act like, a chimpanzee?"

There was a splutter of a laugh from the garage doorway, and Mary Ann turned her head towards Jimmy. But she had to turn it away again quickly before she, too, laughed. It would never do to let Jimmy think she was softening up.

"Don't stand there with your mouth open." Corny was shouting towards Jimmy now. "We've got a job in."

"That!" said Jimmy, moving slowly towards the big cream car. "The American's?"

"Yes, the American's."

"An' she's in for repair?"

"She's in for repair," said Corny.

"And it all happened when you were concentrating on your trombone, Jimmy." This last, said quietly, but with telling emphasis, was from Mary Ann, as she stood at the corner of the building, and, making a deep obeisance with her head, she moved slowly from their view.

Corny and Jimmy exchanged glances; then Jimmy, jerking his head upwards, muttered under his breath, "It's as that American says, she acts like a woman, boss."

"Go on, get on with it."

And Jimmy got on with it. But after a while he said, "You know what, boss? That has something."

"What has?" asked Corny from where he was sitting in the pit under the car. "What you talking about?"

"What the American said: she acts like a woman. It's a punch line, boss. Could make a pop Da-da-da-da-da-daa. She acts like a woo . . . man." He sang the words, and Corny, stopping in the process of unscrewing a nut, closed his eyes, bit on his lip and grinned before bawling, "I'll act like a man if I come up there to you. Get on with it."

5

Mary Ann was sitting at the corner of her dressing-table. She had a pencil in her hand and a sheet of paper in front of her, and she sat looking through the curtains over the road in front of the garage, over the fence and to the far side of Weaver's field, where four men had been moving up and down for a long time, at least all the time she had been sitting here. The far side of Weaver's field was a long way off and she couldn't see what they were doing. But she wasn't very interested; they were only a focal point for her eyes, for her mind was on composing a song.

Last week, after the American had been and left his car, Corny had come upstairs and said, "You know, Jimmy's all there, in this music line, I mean." And she had turned on him scornfully, saying, "Music line! You don't put the word music to the sounds he makes." And to this he had replied, "Well, he's got ideas. Things strike him that wouldn't strike me."

"I should hope so," she had said indignantly; then had added, "He's a nice enough lad, but he's a nit-wit in some ways."

"He's no nit-wit," Corny had protested. "You've got him scared, and that's how he acts with you. You don't know Jimmy. I tell you he's a nice lad, and he's got it up top."

"All right," she had said. "He's a nice lad, but what's struck him that's so brilliant?"

"The title of a song," Corny had said. "The Amer . . . Mr. Blenkinsop said you acted like a woman, you remember? Well, Jimmy said it was a good title for a song, and the more I've been thinking about it the more I agree with him. She acts like a woman. It's like the titles they're having now, the things that are catching on and get into the Top Twenty. So why don't you have a shot at writing the lyrics?"

"What! Write lyrics to, She acts like a woman? Don't be silly."

"Oh, all right, all right. It was only a suggestion. You're always talking about wishing you had something to do, something to occupy your mind at times. And I've told you you should take up your writing again now that you've got time on your hands, with them both away at school. Anyway it was just an idea. Take it or leave it."

He had turned from her and stalked out, and she had looked at the door and exclaimed, "She acts like a woman!" But the words had stuck with her and she had begun to think less scornfully about them when, following Mr. Blenkinsop's return and his generous payment for the hire of the car and the repairs Corny had done, there had been no further work in of any sort for four days.

This morning, their Michael had brought the tractor over and ordered some spares, but they couldn't keep going on family support. It was this that prompted the thought, yet again: if only she could earn some money at home.

Years ago when Corny's hopes were sinking with regard to the prospect of the road, she had started to write furiously, sending off short stories and poems here and there, but they all found their way back to her with "The editor regrets". At the end of a year of hard trying she had to face up to the fact that they would have been better off if she hadn't tried at all, for she had spent much-needed money on postage, paper and a second-hand typewriter.

But this idea of writing ballads, not that she thought the words to some of the pop songs deserved the name of ballad, might have something in it. She had always been good at jingles. But that wasn't enough these days. For a song to really catch on it had to be, well, off-beat.

She had thought that if she could get the tune first she could put the words to it, so she had hummed herself dry for a couple of mornings until she realized that she wasn't any good at original tune building, because most of the songs she was singing in her head were snatches and mixtures of those she heard on the radio and television. So she decided that she would have to stick to the words, and for the last three days she had written hundreds

53

of words, all unknown to Corny. Oh, she wasn't going to let him in on this, although he had given her the lead. She had her own ideas about what she was going to do.

She knew what she wanted. She wanted something with a meaning, something appertaining to life as it was lived to-day, something a bit larger than life, nothing milk and water, or soppy-doppy; that would never go down to-day. It must be virile and about love, and understandable to the teenager, and to her mother and grandmother.

She had almost beaten her head against the wall and given up the whole thing, and then this morning, lying in bed, the words "She acts like a woman" going over and over in her mind, there came to her an idea. But she couldn't do anything about it until she got Corny downstairs and the children out to play. Now she had conveyed her idea in rough rhyme, and it read like this:

SHE ACTS LIKE A WOMAN

SHE ACTS LIKE A WOMAN.
Man, I'm telling you,
SHE ACTS LIKE A WOMAN.
She pelted me with everything,
And then she tore her hair.

SHE ACTS LIKE A WOMAN.
I'd given her my lot,
I was finished, broke,
And then she spoke of love,

SHE ACTS LIKE A WOMAN.
Me, she said,
Me, she wanted,
Not diamonds, mink, or drink,
SHE ACTS LIKE A WOMAN.

I just spread my hands,
What was I to do?
You tell me.
SHE ACTS LIKE A WOMAN.

Early morning, there she stood,
No make-up, face like mud,
And her big eyes raining tears,
And fears.
SHE ACTS LIKE A WOMAN.

Then something moved in here,
Like daylight,
And I could see,
She only wanted me.
SHE ACTS LIKE A WOMAN.

The lead singer would sing the verse, then the rest of the group would come in with "She acts like a woman", and do those falsetto bits. Again she read the words aloud. As it stood, and for what it was, it wasn't bad, she decided. But then, it must have a tune and she wasn't going to send it away to one of those music companies; they might pinch the idea. These things happened. No, it must be set to a tune first, and the only person she could approach who dealt in tunes was . . . Jimmy.

She didn't relish the idea of putting her plan to Jimmy. Still, he was in a group and perhaps one of them could knock up a tune. Of course, if they made the tune up they'd have to share the profits. Well, she supposed half a loaf was better than no bread, and the way things were going down below they'd be lucky if they got half a loaf.

She got slowly to her feet, still staring across the field. She could see her song in the Top Twenty. Young housewife makes the Pop grade, Mary Ann Boyle—she wished it could have been Shaughnessy—jumps from number 19 to number 4. . . . No, number 2, with her "She acts like a woman".

What were they doing over there, those men? Ploughing? Oh no; they could never grow anything in that field, it was full of boulders and outcrops of rock. Her mind, coming down from the heights of fame, concentrated now on the moving figures. What were they doing going up and down? Then screwing her eyes up and peering hard, she realized they were measuring something, measuring the ground.

She took the stairs two at a time.

"Corny! Corny!" She dashed into the office, only to find it empty, then ran into the garage, still calling, and Corny, from the top end, came towards her hurriedly, saying, "What's up? What's up? The bairns?"

"No, no." She shook her head vigorously. "There's something going on in Weaver's field."

"Going on? What?"

"I don't know. I saw them out of the bedroom window, men with a theodolite. They looked like surveyors measuring the ground."

He stared down at her for a moment, then repeated her words again, "Measuring the ground?"

"Yes. Come up and have a look."

They both ran upstairs now and stood at the bedroom window, and after a moment Corny said, "Aye, that's what they're doing all right. But it's yon side, and what for?"

"Perhaps they've been round this side and we haven't heard them. They could have been, you know; they could have been at yon side of the hedge and we wouldn't have seen or heard them."

"They could that," said Corny. "But why? . . . Anyway, whatever they're going to do, you bet your life they'll do at yon side, they wouldn't come over here."

"Aw, don't sound like that." She sought his hand and gripped it.

"Well, it always happens, doesn't it? Look at Riley. He's made a little packet out of the buildings going up at yon side, and he's got a new lot of pumps set up now. I actually see my hands turning green when I pass the place."

She leant her head against him and remained quiet. She, too, turned green when she passed Riley's garage. His garage had been no better than theirs when he started, at least not as good—Riley never kept the place like Corny did—but because of a new estate over there and the factories sprouting up, he had got on like a house on fire. And now Riley acted as if he had been born to the purple; his wife had her own car, and the ordinary schools weren't good enough for the children; two of them were at the

Convent, and the young one at a private school. . . . Would they ever be able to send Rose Mary to the Convent and David . . . ? Her thinking stopped as to where they would send David, and, straightening herself abruptly, she said, "Why don't you take a run round that way and make a few enquiries?"

"It's not a bad idea. But no matter what I find out it won't be that they're going to build this end of the field, for this part's so rock-strewn it even frightens off the speculators."

"Well, go and see."

"Aye, yes, there's no harm in having a look."

He was on the point of turning away from her when he paused, and, gripping her chin in his big hand, he bent down and kissed her, then hurried out of the room.

Mary Ann didn't follow him. There had been a sadness about the kiss and she wanted to cry. The kiss had said, "I'm sorry for the way things have turned out, that my dream was a bubble. I'm sorry for all the things I've deprived you of, I'm sorry for you having to put on that don't-care attitude, and this is the way I want it, when you go to the farm."

"Bust! blast!" The ghost of the old impatient, demanding, I'll-fix-it Mary Ann, came surging up, and she beat the flat of her hand on the dressing-table. Why? Why? He worked like a slave he tried every avenue, he was honest . . . perhaps too honest. But could you be too honest? There was more fiddling in cars than there was in the Hallé Orchestra, and he could have been in on that lucrative racket. Three times he had been approached last year, and from different sources, but he would have none of it. You're a mug, they had said. He had nearly hit one of them who wanted to rent "this forgotten dump", as he had called it, for a place to transform his stolen cars.

Slowly now, she picked up the paper on which she had been writing from the dressing-table. In the excitement of the moment she had forgotten about it. It was a wonder Corny hadn't seen it. At one time he always picked up the pieces of paper lying around, knowing that she had been scribbling.

She heard the Rover start up and saw Corny driving into the lane. After the car had disappeared from view she looked at the sheet of paper in her hand. This would be a good opportunity to tackle Jimmy and see what he thought about the idea.

She was halfway across the room when she stopped. Would he think she was daft? Well, the only way to find out would be to show him what she had written, and she'd better do it now, for Corny wouldn't be long away.

She ran down the back stairs, and when she reached the yard she saw, over the low wall, the children playing in the old car. She waved to them, but they were too engrossed to notice her. She went through the gate, down the path between the beans and potatoes, over a piece of rough ground, to the small door that led into the garage.

"Jimmy!"

Jimmy was sitting on an upturned drum, stranding a length of wire. He raised his head and looked towards her, and said, "Aye, Mrs. Boyle." Then he threw down the wire and came hurrying to her. He liked the boss's wife, although at times when she had her dander up she scared him a bit, but they got on fine. That was until he started practising. Still, he understood, 'cos his mother was the same. She was good-hearted, was the boss's wife, not stingy on the grub. He wished his mother cooked like she did. Cor, the stuff his mother hashed up. . . .

"Aye, Mrs. Boyle, you want me?" He smiled broadly at her.

Mary Ann smiled back at him, and she swallowed twice before she said, "I'd like your advice on something, Jimmy."

". . . My advice, Mrs. . . ."

"Yes. Yes." She shook her head, and her smile widened. "And don't look so surprised." They both laughed sheepishly now, and Mary Ann, taking the folded sheet of paper from her apron pocket, said, in a voice that held a warning, "Now, don't you make game, Jimmy, at what I'm going to tell you, but . . . but I've written some words for a song."

She watched Jimmy's long face stretch to an even longer length, and, perhaps because of the tone of her voice, all he said was, "Aye." He knew she wrote things, the boss had told him, the boss said she was good at it, but a song. He never imagined her writing a song. He thought she was against pop. He said quickly now, "Pop? Pop, is it?"

"Well, sort of. I wondered what you would think of it.

58

Whether you would think it was worth setting to a tune. You know what I mean."

"Aye, aye." He nodded, then held out his hand, and she placed the sheet of paper in it.

"She acts like a woman. Coo! 'cos I said that?" He dug his finger towards the paper. " 'Cos I said that was a good title you've made this up?" He sounded excited; he looked excited; his large mouth was showing all his uneven teeth.

"Yes." She nodded at him. "Mr. Boyle"—she always gave Corny his title when speaking of him to his employee—"Mr. Boyle thought it was a very good title."

"Aye, I think it is an' all, but . . . but you know, it wasn't me who said it in the first place, it was that American, and it just struck me like. . . ."

Time was going on and she didn't want Corny to come back while they were talking. "Read it," she said. She watched Jimmy's eyebrows move upwards as his eyes flicked over the lines, and at one stage he flashed her a look and a wide grin.

When his eyes reached the bottom of the page he took them to the top again and said slowly, "She acts like a woman."

"Well, what do you think?"

"Ee! I think it's great. It's got it, you know, the kind they want. Could I take it and show it to Duke? He's the one that got our group up. He's good at tunes. He can read music an' all; he learned the piano from when he was six. I'll swear he'll like this, 'cos it's got the bull-itch."

Mary Ann opened her mouth and closed it again before she repeated, "Bull-itch? What do you mean, bull-itch?"

"Well, you know." Jimmy tossed his head. "A girl after a fellow."

"Oh, Jimmy."

"Well, that's what they say, Mrs. Boyle. When it's t'other way round they call it the bitchy-itch, an' this 'as really got both."

"Oh, Jimmy. And you think that the words give that impression?"

"Oh, aye. An' they're great. But I didn't know you wrote this stuff, Mrs. Boyle. I bet Duke'll make somethin' of it."

"Oh, if only he could, Jimmy. And then we'll get together and see about getting it recorded and trying for the Top Twenty."

She could have sworn that Jimmy's face dropped half its length again. "Top Twenty?" His voice was high in his head. "But, Mrs. Boyle, you don't get into the Top Twenty unless you've got a manager and things, like the Beatles, and we're just startin' so to speak. Well, I mean, I am; I'm the worst, among the players, that is." He lowered his head.

"What do the others do?" asked Mary Ann, flatly now.

"Well, Duke can play most things a bit; Barny, he plays the drums; and Poodle, he's best on the cornet. But he's on the flute now, and Dave has the guitar."

"What do you call yourselves?" asked Mary Ann.

"Oh, nowt yet. We've been thinkin' about it, but we've not come up with anythin' yet, not anythin' catchy. You want somethin' different, you do, don't you?"

"Yes," said Mary Ann. "I'll think up something."

"Aw." Jimmy's face was straight now. "Duke'll want to see to that; he's good on thinkin' up titles and things."

There was a pause; then Mary Ann said, "You'll have to bring Duke along to see me."

"Aye, I will," said Jimmy. "He'll be tickled, I think."

"Jimmy."

"Aye, Mrs. Boyle."

"I don't want you to say anything to Mr. Boyle about this."

"No?"

"No. It might come to nothing, you see."

Jimmy looked puzzled, then said, "Well, even if it doesn't, it'll still be a bit of fun."

Mary Ann wanted to say that at this stage she wasn't out for fun, she was out for money, but she was afraid Jimmy wouldn't understand, so all she said was, "Don't speak of it to Mr. Boyle till I tell you, will you not?"

"O.K., Mrs. Boyle, just as you say."

"And when you bring Duke along, tell him not to say anything either."

"Will do, Mrs. Boyle, will do."

"Thanks, Jimmy." She smiled at him. And he smiled at her; then watched her go out through the little door.

Well, would you believe that, her writin' things like that. He looked down at the paper and read under his breath: "I'd given her my lot. I was finished, broke and then she spoke of love. She acts like a woman." He lifted his head and looked towards the door again. It was as Duke was always sayin', you never could tell. . . .

6

Rose Mary, from her position on top of the car, saw her mother come out of the garage and go into their back yard, and she called to her "O-Oo, Mam!" but her mother didn't turn round. Perhaps she hadn't called loud enough.

Oh, it was hot. She clambered down from the roof, saying to David, "I'm going to lie in the grass, it's too hot. Come on."

When they were both lying in the grass, she said, "I wish we could go to the sands at Shields. If Greatgran McBride lived in Shields instead of Greatgran McMullen we would go more often. I don't like Greatgran McMullen, do you?" She turned her head and looked at David, and David, looking skywards, shook his head.

She wished it wasn't so hot; she wished she had an ice-cream. She wished they could go on a holiday. Peter had gone on a holiday. He was going to come and play with them when he came back, but that would be a long time, nearly three weeks. He had said the other day that he would rather stay here and play on the car. He liked playing with them. . . . Oh, it was hot. They had only broken up for the holidays three days ago and she wished she was back at school. . . . No, she didn't, 'cos last week had been awful. Miss Plum had been awful right from the Monday following the Sunday when she had taken their David to sit beside her. Nothing had gone right from then. And Father Carey had messed things up an' all. She had gone to school on the Monday knowing that something would happen because Father Carey was a good pray-er. And things did happen, but not the way she wanted them to, because they had hardly got in the classroom before Miss Plum collared their David and put him in the front seat right under her nose, and David didn't let a squeak out of him. He usually squawked when anybody took him away from her, but he didn't squawk at Miss Plum. She waited all morning for him to squawk, or do something. It was nearly dinner-time before she realized that Miss Plum had got at Father Carey before she had, and that he was doing it her way.

Oh, it was hot. Oh, it was. And she hated Miss Plum, oh, she did. And she didn't like Father Carey very much either. Ee! She would get wrong for thinking like that. Well, she couldn't help it. She had thought it without thinkin'. And she hadn't made her first confession yet, so she wouldn't have to tell it, so that was all right.

Her mam said when she was a little girl she took all her troubles to Father Owen and he sorted them out for her. She wished she could go and see Father Owen, but he lived far away in Jarrow.

Aw, it was hot.

"Come on." She pulled herself up and put out her hand. "I'm goin' in for a drink."

She was too hot to do any shouting on the back stairs, and she was in the kitchen before she opened her mouth. And then she closed it quickly because her ma and da were talking, dark talking. She knew she hadn't to interrupt when they were dark talking. They dark talked at night-time when she was in bed, and if she tried hard enough she could hear what they said. Usually, it made her sad, or just sorry like. And now the tones of their voices told her they were dark talking again. Her ma looked sad and her da's face was straight, and her da was saying, "Sort of winded me like, to see him sitting there talking to Riley and the car standing near the pumps. I thought he liked what I did to the car and I just charged him the minimum. I didn't put a penny extra on because he was an American, and he seemed over the moon at the time. But that's over a week ago; and when he didn't show up this week I thought he had gone on. But there he was, at Riley's garage."

Rose Mary watched her mother look down towards her feet, and she wanted to say to her, "Can I have a drink, Mam?" But she didn't, 'cos her mam was taking no notice of her.

"What's he doing in these parts, anyway?" said Mary Ann now.

63

"I don't know, I didn't like to probe. And a funny thing, unless I'm vastly mistaken, the car he had to-day, although it was a cream one, wasn't the same one as he brought here the other day."

"But he can't have two cars like that?"

"A fellow like him could have three, or half-a-dozen."

"But how could you tell the difference when you were just passing?"

"Oh, you notice things quick when you're dealing with cars. This one hadn't so much chrome on, but it was as big. I noticed, too, that the boot was open a bit and the end of a long, narrow case was sticking out, like the end of a golf bag, only it couldn't have been a golf bag 'cos that boot would take ten golf bags. Anyway, it looked chock-a-block, as if he was all packed up to go . . . so, that's that."

"And you didn't find out about the men in the field?"

"No, I stopped before I got to Riley's and tried to find a place over the hedge to look through, but it's a tangled mess down there. But I did ask a scavenger, but he could tell me nothing. And well, after I passed the garage I didn't bother, the wind seemed knocked out of me. It was a funny feeling. I mean about the American. I really thought as long as he was in these parts he would come here."

The silence that fell on the kitchen was too much for Rose Mary, and besides she had that sorry feeling seeing her dad and her mam with their heads bent and she wanted to cry. She said softly, "We're dry, Mam; can we have a fizzy drink? Lemon?"

"What? Oh, yes. Just a minute." Mary Ann turned away and went into the scullery, and Rose Mary went and stood close against her father's leg, and, taking his limp fingers in hers, she looked up at him, and said, "I hate that American."

"Rose Mary!" His voice was sharp now. "You're not to say such things. Mr. Blenkinsop was very kind to you."

"Well, I don't want him to be kind, I hate him. An' David hates him an' all. Don't you, David?" She looked to where David was stretched out on the floor, and David turned his head lazily towards her and moved it downwards.

64

"Stop it!" Corny now bent down, and, his face close to hers, he said, "Now look, Rose Mary. You don't have to hate everybody that doesn't do what you want them to do, understand? And David doesn't hate the . . . Mr. Blenkinsop. Who bought you the ice-cream and lollies last week? Mr. Blenkinsop gave you that money, and don't forget it."

There came to them now a distant tingling sound, and Mary Ann called from the scullery, "That's the phone, I think." And when she came into the kitchen with the two glasses of fizzy lemon water, Corny was gone. As she handed one glass to Rose Mary and one to David, Rose Mary said, "I do hate that American."

"You heard what your father said to you, didn't you?"

"Well, he's buying his petrol from Riley's."

"He can buy his petrol anywhere he likes."

"Our petrol's better than Riley's."

Mary Ann closed her eyes and turned away.

"It is."

"Rose Mary!"

"If I had that pound note I'd give it him back."

"Rose Mary!"

"Mary Ann!"

Hearing Corny's voice calling up the front stairs, Mary Ann hurried out of the room and on to the landing, and, looking down at him, she said, "What is it?"

"Prepare yourself."

"What's happened? What's the matter now?"

"Michael's just phoned. Your grannie's on her way here."

"Me grannie coming here!"

"So Michael thinks."

"But why? Is she at the farm?"

"No, she was there on Sunday. But Michael was driving back from Jarrow and at the traffic lights he happened to glance up at the bus, and there she was sitting, and, as he said, you couldn't mistake the old girl. Busby an' all."

"But how does he know she's coming here?"

"Well, she was on the Gateshead bus, and she doesn't get that one to go to the farm, so he put two and two together and got off at the first telephone box and broke the news. He thought you would like to be prepared."

"Oh, no. I only wanted this. . . . But why is she coming, and at this time in the day? It must be two years since she was here."

"Well, get the bairns changed." Corny's voice was soft now, soothing. "And put your armour on, and smile."

"Aw, Corny." Mary Ann's voice, too, was low, but it had a desperate sound. Her grannie. The last person she wanted to see at any time. "Corny, look." Her voice was rapid. "What about me taking them out for the day? You could tell her we've gone to the sands."

"It's no use. From the time Michael phoned, the bus could be at the bottom of the road by now, and you could just run into her, even if you were ready. . . . Stick it out; you're a match for her."

"Not any longer, I haven't got the energy."

"Wait till you see her, it'll inject you with new life." He smiled up at her, then turned away, and she stood for a moment looking down the stairs, before moving swiftly back in the room.

"Hurry up and finish your drinks," she said, "and come on into the bathroom."

"We goin' to have a bath again, Mam? We had one last——"

"I only want you to wash your face and hands and put on your blue print, the one with the smocking."

"We going to the sands?"

"No." Mary Ann called now from the landing. "Your great-gran's coming."

"Me great-gran?" Rose Mary was running out of the room on to the landing, and David was behind her now. "Which one?"

"McMullen."

"Aw, not her, Mam."

"Yes, her. Come on now." Mary Ann pulled them both into the bathroom. "Get your things off and you wash your face and hands, I'll see to David."

David had never been washed and changed so rapidly in his life. When he was attired in clean pants and tee-shirt he stood watching his mother jumping out of one dress and into another, and then, with Rose Mary, he was hustled back into the living-room and ordered to sit. He sat, and Rose Mary sat, and while they waited they watched their mother flying round the room, pushing their toys into the bottom of the cupboard, tidying up the magazines, putting a bit of polish on the table, even rubbing a wash leather over the lower panes of the window, and she had only cleaned the window yesterday. At last Rose Mary was forced to volunteer, "Perhaps she's fallen down, Mam?"

Oh, if only she had. Mary Ann groaned inside. If only she had fallen into the ditch and broken her leg. How gladly she would call the ambulance and see her whisked away. But her grannie wouldn't fall into a ditch and break her leg. Nothing adverse would happen to her grannie; her grannie would live to torment her family until she was a hundred, perhaps a hundred and ten. She could never see her grannie dying. Her grannie was like all the evil in the world. As long as there were people there would be evil. As long as there was a Shaughnessy left there would be Grannie McMullen to torment them.

"Mary Ann! You've got a visitor." It was Corny's voice from the bottom of the stairs, and Mary Ann, turning about, walked across the room. But she paused near Rose Mary's chair to say, "Now mind, behave yourself. I don't want any repeat of that Sunday at the farm. You remember?"

Her words were like an echo from the past, like an echo of Lizzie saying to her, "Now mind yourself, don't cheek your grannie, I'm warning you." She opened the door and went on to the landing and said, "Who is it?" Then she made a suitable pause before adding, "Oh, hello, Gran."

Mrs. McMullen was coming unassisted up the steep stairs, and when she reached the top she stood panting slightly, looking at Mary Ann, and Mary Ann looked at her.

Ever since she first remembered seeing her grannie she hadn't seemed to change by one wrinkle or hair. Her hair was still black and abundant, and as always supported a large hat, a black straw to-day. Her small, dark eyes still held their calculating devilish gleam. The skin of her face was covered with the tracery of lines not detectable unless under close scrutiny, so she looked much younger than her seventy-six years. She was wearing this morning an up-to-date light-weight grey check coat which yelled aloud in comparison to the hair style and hat adorning it.

"It's warm to-day," said Mary Ann.

"Warm! It's bakin', if you ask me. And the walk from the bus doesn't make it any better. I would have thought that after being stuck miles from civilization afore you married you would have plumped for some place nearer the town. But I suppose beggars can't be choosers. . . . Aw, let me sit down, off me feet."

"Let your grannie sit down." Mary Ann was nodding towards Rose Mary, and Rose Mary, sliding off the dining-room chair, stood to one side, and as Mary Ann watched her grannie seat herself she thought, "Beggars can't be choosers. Oh, what I'd like to say to her."

"I'll get you a cup of tea." Mary Ann moved towards the scullery now, and Mrs. McMullen, without turning her head, said, "There's time enough for that; I'll have something cold if it's not too much trouble. . . . Well now." Mrs. McMullen put her hands up slowly to her hat and withdrew the pin, and as she did so she looked at the children. First at Rose Mary, then at David, then to Rose Mary again, and she said, "You underweight?"

"What?"

Rose Mary screwed up her face at her great-grandmother.

"I said are you underweight? And don't say 'What?' Say, 'What, Great-gran?' Do you get weighed at school?"

"Yes."

"Didn't they tell you you were underweight?"

"No . . . no, Great-gran."

"Well, if my eyes don't deceive me, that's what they should have done."

"I've brought you a lemon drink."

"Oh . . . thanks. I was just saying to her"—Mrs. McMullen nodded to her great-grandchild—"she looks underweight. Anything wrong with her?"

"No, no, nothing. She's as healthy as an ox." Mary Ann was determined that nothing that this old devil said would make her rise.

She watched the old woman take a long drink from the glass,

68

then put her hand in her pocket and bring out a folded white handkerchief with which she wiped her mouth. And then she watched her turn her attention to David. "Hello there," she said.

David looked back at this funny old woman. He looked deep into her eyes, and his own darkened and he grinned. He grinned widely at her.

"He not talking yet?"

Mary Ann hesitated for a long moment before saying, "He's making progress."

"Is he talking or isn't he?"

Steady, steady. Metaphorically speaking, Mary Ann gripped her own shoulder. "He can say certain words. The teacher's very pleased with him, isn't she, Rose Mary?"

"Yes, yes, he's Miss Plum's favourite. She takes him to the front of the class and she pins up his drawings."

"They only have to do that with idiots."

The words had been muttered below her breath but they were clear to Mary Ann, if not to the children. As Rose Mary asked, "What did you say, Great-gran?" Mary Ann had to turn away. She went into the scullery, and as her mother had done many many times in her life, and for the same reason, she stood leaning against the draining-board gripping its edge. She longed, in this moment, for Lizzie's support, and she realized that this was only the second time that she had battled with her grannie on her own; there had always been someone to check her tongue, or even her hand. On her grannie's only other visit here two years ago, she'd had the support of their Michael and Sarah, but now she was on her own, and she didn't trust herself. How long would she stay? Would she stay for dinner? Very likely. But Corny would be here then, and Corny could manage her somehow. She had found she couldn't rile him, consequently she didn't get at him. She was even pleasant to him; the nasty things she had to say she said behind his back.

She almost jumped back into the kitchen as she heard her grannie say, "Be quiet, child. Give him a chance, let him answer for himself."

"I was only sayin'——"

69

"I know what you were saying." Mrs. McMullen now turned her head up towards Mary Ann. "This one"—she thumbed Rose Mary—"is the spit of you, you know, she doesn't know when to stop. I don't think you'll get him talkin' as long as he's got the answers ready made for him."

Mary Ann forced herself not to bow her head, and not to lower her eyes from her grannie's. It was galling to think that this dreadful old woman was advocating the same remedy for David's impediment as Corny and her mother. Mrs. McMullen now turned her eyes away from Mary Ann, saying with a sigh, "Aw well, it's your own business. And you'd never take advice, as long as I can remember . . . I think I'll take me coat off, it's enough to roast you in here. I'd open the window."

"The window's open." Mary Ann took her grannie's coat and went out of the room with it, and laid it on the bed in the bedroom. And now she stood leaning against the bed-rail trying to calm herself before returning to the room. The old devil, the wicked old devil. And she was wicked—vicious and wicked. On the bedroom chimney-breast hung a portrait of Corny and her on their wedding day, and her mind was lifted to the moment when they were walking down from the altar and her grannie stole the picture by falling into the aisle in a faint; and in that moment, that wonderful, wonderful moment when all her feelings should have been good, and her thoughts even holy, she had wished, as she saw them carrying her grannie away down the aisle, that she'd peg out. Yes, such was the effect her grannie had on her that on the altar steps she had wished a thing like that.

When she returned to the kitchen it was to hear Mrs. McMullen saying to Rose Mary, "But how many in a week, how many cars does he work on in a week?" and Rose Mary replying, "Oh, lots, dozens."

"Does he get much work in?" Mrs. McMullen's gimlet eyes met Mary Ann's as she came across the room.

"Who? Corny?" Her voice was high, airy. "Oh, yes, he gets plenty of work in."

"Well!" The word was said on a long, exhaling breath. "It must be his oft time, for what I could see when I passed the

70

garage was space, empty space, and the floor as clean as a whistle. . . . Why doesn't he sell up? I heard your father on about him having an offer."

"Oh, yes, yes, he's had offers, but he doesn't want to sell up, we're quite content here."

Her da on about them having an offer. Her grannie must have been saying something to her mother and her da had made it up on the spur of the moment about them having an offer. That's what he would do. Good for her da.

Mary Ann said now, as she brought the tray to the delf-rack and took down some cups and saucers, "We did consider one offer we had, but then it's so good for the children out here, plenty of fresh air and space, and the house is comfortable."

"You can't live on fresh air and space. As for comfort . . ." Mrs. McMullen looked round the room. "You want something bigger than this with them growing, you couldn't swing a cat in it."

"Well, we don't happen to have a . . ." Mary Ann abruptly checked her words, and so hard did she grip the cup in her hand that she wouldn't have been surprised if it had splintered into fragments. There, her grannie had won. She put the sugar basin and milk jug quietly on to the tray and took it to the table under the window before saying, "It suits us. I'm happy here. We're all happy here."

"Your mother doesn't seem to think so."

"What!" Mary Ann swung round and looked at the back of her grannie's head. "My mother would never say I was unhappy. She couldn't say it, because I'm not unhappy."

"She doesn't have to say it. She happens to be my daughter, I know what she's thinking, I know how she views the set-up."

Mary Ann again went into the scullery and again she was holding the draining-board, and she bit on her lip now, almost drawing blood. It was at this moment that Rose Mary joined her and, clutching her dress at the waist, she looked up at her. Her ma was upset, her ma was nearly crying. She hated her great-gran, she was an awful great-gran. She whispered now, brokenly, "Don't cry, Mam. Aw, don't cry, Mam."

"I'm not crying." Mary Ann had brought her face down to

71

her daughter's as she whispered. "Go back into the room and be nice. Go on. Go on now for me."

"Aw, but Mam."

"Go on."

Rose Mary dutifully went into the room and took her seat again, but she did not look at her great-grandmother.

"What are you doing at school?"

When silence greeted Mrs. McMullen's question, David turned his bright gaze on his sister, and when she didn't answer he moved quickly to her and shook her arm, and for the first time in her life she pushed off his hand, and Mrs. McMullen, quick to notice the action, said, "You needn't be nasty to him, he was only telling you to answer in the only way he knew."

Now Rose Mary was looking at her great-grandmother and, the spirit of her mother rising in her, she said, "I don't like you."

"Ah-ha! Here we go again, another generation of 'em. So you don't like me? Well, I'll not lose any sleep over that."

"I like me Great-gran McBride."

Mrs. McMullen's face darkened visibly. "Oh, you do, do you? And I hope you like her beautiful house, and her smell."

"Yes, yes, I do. And David does an' all. We like goin' there, I'd go there all the time. I like me Great-gran McBride."

"Rose Mary!" Mary Ann was speaking quietly from the scullery door, and Rose Mary, now unable to control her tears, slid to her feet, crying, "Well, I do like me Great-gran McBride, I do, Mam. You know I do."

"Yes, I know, but now be quiet. Behave yourself, and stop it."

"I don't like her, I don't, Mam." Rose Mary, her arm outstretched, was pointing at Mrs. McMullen.

"Rose Mary!" As Mary Ann advanced towards her, Rose Mary backed towards the door, staring at her great-grandmother all the while, and as she groped behind her and found the handle she bounced her head towards the old lady, saying, "I'll never like you 'cos you're nasty." Then, turning about, she ran out of the room and down the stairs.

She'd find her dad, she would, and tell him. Her great-gran was awful, she was a pig, she'd made her mam cry, she'd tell her dad and he would go up and give her one for making her mam cry.

She ran to the garage, but she couldn't see her dad. But through her tears she saw a big car standing in the mouth of the garage and another car at the top end with Jimmy working on it. She ran out of the garage again and went towards the office, but she stopped just outside the door. Somebody was talking to her dad, and she recognized his voice. It was that nasty American who bought his petrol from Riley's.

"Rose Mary!" It was her mother's voice coming from the stairs. She looked round before running again. She wasn't going to go upstairs and sit with her great-gran, she wasn't. She hated her great-gran. She would hide. Yes, that's what she would do, she would hide. She looked wildly round her. And then she saw a good hiding place and darted towards it. . . .

7

In the office, Corny leant against his desk, mostly for support, as he stared down at the American sitting in the one seat provided. "I can't quite take it in," he said.

Mr. Blenkinsop smiled with one corner of his mouth higher than the other. "Give yourself time," he replied. "Give yourself time."

"May I ask what made you change your mind, I mean to build your factory at this side instead of yon side?"

"You may, and I'll tell you. But it won't do you any good. I mean it won't help you any further, for you've already reached the stage when you know that it's best in the long run to play fair."

Corny screwed up his eyes as he surveyed Mr. Blenkinsop. He had always played fair in business, but he wondered where he came in in the American's plan in this line, but he waited.

"As I told you, my father built up Blenkinsop's from making boxes in a house yard, with my three brothers and six sisters all rounded up to help in the process, cutting, nailing, getting orders, delivering. It was before the last war and things were bad. I was just a youngster, but my father thought I had what it took to sell, and so I was put on to do the rounds going from door to door in the better-class neighbourhood of our town, showing them samples of our fancy-made boxes to put their Christmas presents in, the kind of presents that we kids only dreamed of. From the beginning it was, as our father said, small profit and quick return. 'Put into your work,' he said, 'more than you expect to get back in clear cash and the profits will mount up for you.' You know, that took a bit of working out to us boys whose only thought was to make money, and fast, but after a time we understood that if you make your product good enough

74

it will sell itself a thousandfold, and in the end your profits will be high. . . . Well, after the war the business went like a house on fire. We were all in it, those of us who were left. Three died in the war, my three brothers, but the girls and their husbands still carry on their end of it, and our father's maxim still holds good."

Corny shook his head, but he still did not quite follow, and the American knew this, and he lit a cigarette and offered Corny one before he went on, "It's like this. I have two cars. I brought one to you, and I took one to Mr. Riley. I knew exactly what was wrong with each; in fact, the same was wrong in both cases. Mr. Riley charged me almost fifty per cent more than you did, and he bodged the job, at least his mechanics did. I guessed he'd put on twenty per cent in any case, me being an American and rolling. They think we are all rolling. But to pile on fifty per cent . . . Oh no. No. So I made a call on Mr. Riley this morning and told him I thought he had slightly overcharged me. He was, what you call, I think, shirty. In any case, Mr. Riley thought he'd got it all in the pan. He knew I had bought this whole piece of land a month ago, and as he said, only a fool would think of building this end, for just look at the stuff they would have to move, rock going deep. Well, he got a little surprise this morning when I told him it was on this end I had decided to put my factory, at least the main gates of it. My storehouses will now back on to the far road, there will be main gates leading to the main road, and another at the far end of this road leading to your Gateshead, but I'm putting my main building towards the end of your road, here. . . . Oh no"—he raised his hand and waved it back and forward—"not entirely to help you, but because it is advantageous, as I see it, to my plan. As I've told you, seeing the material we're dealing with I don't want petrol stores too near to the works, but I want them near enough to be convenient for the lorries and cars, and from the first I saw I had the choice of two petrol stations, and I've made it. The fifty per cent supercharge finally decided me which of the two men I preferred to deal with. That's how I do business. I look over the ground first—panning for gold dust my father used to call it. Always look for the gold and

the dirt will drop through the riddle, he would say. . . . Well."
Mr. Blenkinsop surveyed Corny. "There it is."

"Well, sir, I'm . . . I'm flabbergasted."

"Oh." The American put his head back. "That's a wonderful word, flabbergasted." He rose to his feet. "We'll do business together, young man." He put his hand on Corny's shoulder, much as a father would, and said quietly, "You leave this to me now. You'll need money for more pumps; we'll want a lot of petrol because our fleet of lorries won't be small. There'll be a great many private cars, too, as nearly all the workers in England have cars now; it isn't an American prerogative any longer." He smiled. "How much land did you say you had to the side of you, I mean your own?"

"Just over three-quarters of an acre. It runs back for about four hundred feet though; it's a narrow strip."

"Good, you'll need every bit of it. You'll want workshops and a place for garaging cars. That's a good idea." He made for the door now. Then, turning abruptly, he said, "What's kept you here for seven years, in this dead end?"

"Hope. Hoping for the road going through; hoping for a day like this . . . someone like you, sir."

"Well, all I can say is that I admire your tenacity; it would have daunted many a stronger man. You know, you with your knowledge of cars would likely have made a much better living working in one of the big garages."

"I know that, sir, but I've always wanted to be my own boss."

The American surveyed him with a long, penetrating glance, then, punching him gently in the shoulder, he said, "You'll always be your own boss, son. Never you fear that. But now . . ." He stepped out of the door, saying, "I've got a mixed week-end before me, business and pleasure. I'm off to Doncaster to see a cousin of mine, who'll be on the board of the new concern. Also, I hope to persuade him to be my general manager. I should be back on Monday, and then we will get round the table and talk about ways and means." He took two steps forward and half-glanced over his shoulder and said, "You wouldn't like me to buy you out?"

Corny stopped behind him. He could see only a part of the American's profile; he didn't know what expression was on his face, whether this was a test or not; but he said immediately, "No, sir, I wouldn't like you to buy me out. I don't want anybody to buy me out; I want to work my business up."

"Good." Mr. Blenkinsop moved on again towards the garage, saying, "And I haven't the slightest doubt that our arrangement will go well."

"Nor me, sir. I've always liked working with Americans."

Mr. Blenkinsop stopped and turned fully round now. "You've worked with Americans before?"

"Yes, I was in America for close on a year, just outside New York."

"Well, I'll be jiggered. And you never opened your mouth about it?"

"Well, sir, I didn't think it would be of any interest to you; you must meet thousands of people who have been in America."

"Yes, and they always start by telling me just that. What were you doing over there?"

"Oh, I first of all worked on the ground floor in Flavors."

"Flavors! The car people?"

"Yes. And then I did a bit in the office, and got into the showrooms."

"All in under a year?" Mr. Blenkinsop's eyes were now slits of disbelief, and Corny, lowering his head, said, "It was influence, sir."

"Ah! Ah! I see. But why didn't you stay on?"

"Well, just as I said a minute ago, I wanted to be me own boss, go on my own road. I wouldn't turn down help, but I didn't want to be carried, and in this particular case I wasn't being carried for meself; it was . . . well, it's a long story, sir, but it was because of my wife. There's an old gentleman—he's the owner of the farm her father manages. He's very fond of her, and between you and me he wanted to get me out of her way; he had other ideas for her."

The American's head went back and he let out a bellow of a laugh. "And you beat him to it by coming back. Good for you. You know"—his chin was forward once more—"I wouldn't like

77

to come up against you in a fight, business or otherwise. I've an idea I'd lose."

"Aw, sir." Corny, laughing too, now, moved his head from side to side.

"Well, anyway, I'm glad to know you've been to America. But tell me, did you like it there?"

"Oh, yes, sir. I liked it, and the people, but I was missing Mary Ann . . . my wife."

"The one that acts like a woman?" Again there was laughter. "Well, you did right to come back. Now I'd better be off. And you go and tell your wife the good news. . . . Well, I hope you consider it good news."

Corny opened the car door for Mr. Blenkinsop. Then, closing it, and bending down, he said, "Quite truthfully, sir, I'm dazed."

"You won't remain in that state long. I'm speaking from experience. You'll take the breaks good and bad, in your stride. You'll see." They smiled at each other. Corny straightened up, then watched the car backing out of the garage. He followed it as it turned out of the drive, and he answered Mr. Blenkinsop's wave with a lift of his big arm.

Lord! Lord! Could he believe it? Could he? That his luck had changed at last? He had the desire to drop down on his knees and give thanks, but, instead, he turned round and pelted back across the drive, through the house door and up the stairs, and, bursting into the room, he came to a dead stop. Aw, lor, he'd forgotten about old bitterguts! But why not spill the good news into her lap as way of repayment for all she had put Mary Ann through for marrying him, and before that? "Mary Ann!" He shouted as if she were on a fell top, and she came to the scullery door wide-eyed, saying, "What's wrong?"

It was funny, he thought, that whenever they shouted at each other they always thought there was something wrong. In a few strides he was across the little kitchen, and, his arms under her armpits, he hoisted her upwards as if she was a child, and before the amazed gaze of her grannie he swung her around, then set her to the floor. But, still holding her with one hand, he bent and lifted David on to his shoulders, and, like this, he

78

looked down at Mrs. McMullen and cried, "Behold! You see a successful man, Gran."

"You gone barmy?"

"Yes, I've gone barmy."

"Well, it's either that or you're drunk."

"I'm both. I'm barmy and I'm drunk." He pressed Mary Ann to his side until she almost cried out with the pressure on her ribs. Something has happened, something good. But what? The road? She looked up at him and said in awe-filled tones, "Corny. The road . . . the road's going through?"

He looked down at her, and, still shouting, he said, "No, not the road . . . the American."

She tried to pull away from him. "The American? What you talking about?"

"He's building a factory right at our door, this side of the field, and Bob Quinton's got the job. But he's contracting me to supply all the petrol, and much more, oh, much more, cars, garaging, repairs . . . the lot . . . the lot. What do you think of that?" He was not looking at Mary Ann now but bending towards Mrs. McMullen, and that undauntable dame looked back at him and said, "I wouldn't count me chickens afore they are hatched; there's many a hen sat on a nest of pot eggs."

"Oh, you're the world's little hopeful, aren't you, Gran?" He was still bending towards her, with David holding on to his hair with his fists to save himself from slipping, and Mary Ann, now pulling away from him, stood with her hands joined under her chin, and, forgetting about her grannie, forgetting about everything but Corny and the American, she said, "Oh, Corny! Oh, Corny! Thank God. Thank God."

"Humility. Humility. Thanking God. You must be cracking up."

"Gran!" Mary Ann looked towards the set-faced old woman. "You couldn't upset me if you tried. Go on. Think up the worst that's in you, and I'll fling my arms around you and hug you."

Mary Ann was surprised at her own words, as was Mrs. McMullen. The old lady was evidently taken aback for a moment, but only for a moment, before she said, "I wouldn't do any such thing. I'm an old woman and the shock might be the finish of me; for you to show me any affection would be more than me heart could stand, the last straw in fact."

Corny and Mary Ann looked at each other; then they laughed, and Corny, reaching out an arm, pulled Mary Ann once more into his embrace, and said, "I would like to take you out this minute and give you a slap-up meal. What've you got in? What's for dinner? All of a sudden, I'm ravenous."

"Some ham and salad and a steamed pud, that's all. But we'll have a drink, eh? Go on. Put him down." She laughed up at David, who laughed back at her. Then, pulling herself from Corny, she ran towards the scullery, but paused at the door to call over her shoulder, "Go and bring Rose Mary."

"Rose Mary? Aw, where is she?" Corny looked about him.

"Oh, she went downstairs a little while ago, about ten minutes ago. She'll likely be in the old car."

Corny took his son from his shoulder and put him on the floor, and he didn't enquire why Rose Mary had gone out without David, for he fancied he knew the reason. The old girl had likely upset her, as she had done her mother so many times in the years gone by.

He ran down the back stairs and looked towards the old car and called, "Rose Mary! Rose Mary!" And when he didn't receive an answer he went into the garage and there saw Jimmy at the far end. Oh, he would have to tell Jimmy the news. Oh, yes, he must tell Jimmy.

It took a full five minutes to tell Jimmy, and all the time Jimmy, bashing one fist against the other, could only say, "Ee, boss! Coo, boss! No, boss! You don't say, boss!"

Then as Corny bent his long length to go out of the top door to the back of the garage again, Jimmy called to him, "Does that mean I'll get a rise, boss?"

Twisting round, Corny grinned at him. "It could," he said. "It just could."

"Good-oh, boss."

Corny now ran across the field towards the old car. He wanted to hold his daughter, to throw her sky high and cry, "We're going places, my Rose Mary, we're going places. And you're going to a good school, me girl." He wanted to get into his car and fly to the farm and yell to Mike, "I've done it, Mike. It's come, Mike." And Mike would understand, and he would thump him on the back. And Michael would thump him on the back, and Sarah would hold his hands and say, "I'm glad for you both." . . . . But what would Lizzie say? Perhaps Lizzie wouldn't be so pleased, because her eyes had always said to her daughter, "Well, I told you so." And then there was Mr. Lord. Mr. Lord, who had offered him the bribe of Baxter's up-to-date garage, not to help him personally but so that he would be able to afford to keep his wife in the way that Mr. Lord thought she should be kept, the way she would have been kept if she had married his grandson, the way Lettice was kept now. Aw, he would go to him and say. . . . What would he say? He stopped at the end of the field. He would say nothing; he would just let time speak for him; he had a long way to go yet but the road was going through. Oh boy, yes. A different road to what he thought, but, nevertheless, a road.

"Rose Mary!" he shouted towards the car; and again "Rose Mary!" She was hiding from him, the little monkey.

When he got to the car he saw at a glance she wasn't there. He returned to the garage, calling all the way, "Rose Mary! Rose Mary!"

"Jimmy."

"Yes, boss?"

"You seen Rose Mary?"

"No, boss, not since the pair of them were on the old car."

Corny stood at the opening to the garage, looking about him, and spoke over his shoulder to Jimmy, saying, "That was some time ago. She's been upstairs since, and came down."

"Where's David?" Jimmy had come to his side now.

"Oh, he's upstairs; their great-grandmother's come. She upset Rose Mary and she came downstairs. She must be hiding somewhere."

"But where could she be hiding, boss?"

Corny looked at Jimmy. He looked at him for about ten seconds before swinging round. Yes, where could she be hiding? He now ran round to the back of the house and opened the coal-house door, and the doors of the two store-houses; then, dashing up the back stairs, he burst into the kitchen, saying, "Has she come in?"

"Rose Mary?" Mary Ann turned from the table. "No, I told you, she's out."

"She's not about anywhere."

"But she must be somewhere." Mary Ann moved slowly towards Corny and stared up into his face as he said, "I've looked everywhere."

"Perhaps . . . perhaps she's gone for a walk up the road." Her voice was small.

She'd never go up the road without him. Corny slowly drooped his head in the direction of David, who was standing stiffly staring at them, his eyes wide, his mouth slightly open.

"Take the car," said Mary Ann quietly, "and go to both ends of the road."

"Yes, yes." Corny nodded quickly, and as quickly turned about and went out of the room and down the stairs.

As Mary Ann looked towards her grannie, thinking, "It's her fault; she's to blame; she scared her, as she did me for years," David made a sound. It was high, and it sounded like Romary. Mary Ann, moving swiftly towards him, caught him to her, and he clutched at her dress, crying again, higher this time, on the verge of a scream, "Romary!"

"It's all right, darling." Mary Ann lifted him up into her arms. "Daddy's gone to fetch Rose Mary. It's all right; it's all right."

"Romary."

Mary Ann stared into the eyes of her son, glistening now with tears. Romary he had said. It wasn't a far cry to Rose Mary. She pressed him closer to her.

"She wants her backside smacked."

Mary Ann hitched David to one side in her arms so that she could confront her grannie squarely. "She doesn't want her backside smacked, and she's not going to get her backside smacked, wherever she is."

"That's right, break her neck with softness. It's been done before." The old woman's gimlet eyes raked Mary Ann up and down.

82

"How I bring up my children is my business. . . ."

"Oh, now, don't start. You were acting like an angel coming down by parachute a minute ago, and now you're getting back to normal."

"Look, Gran. I don't want to fight with you."

"Who's fightin', I ask you? Who starts the fights?"

"As far back as I remember, you have."

"Well, I like that. I like that. I come here, all this way in the baking heat, and that's what I get. Well, I should have known. I've had so much experience, I should have known." The big, bushy head was moving in wide sweeps now, and Mrs. Mc-Mullen, pulling herself to her feet, said, "Get me me coat."

Mary Ann didn't say, "Aw, Gran, don't be silly. Stay and have a bite of dinner." No. She put David down and marched out of the room, and returned a minute later with the coat in her hand. She did not attempt to help her grannie on with it; she just handed it to her, for she couldn't bear to touch her.

"There." Mrs. McMullen pulled on the coat. "Wonderful, isn't it? The kindness of people. I'm going out the way I come, without bite or sup, except for a drop of watery lemonade. I've got a long journey ahead of me afore I reach home, and I could collapse on the way. . . . But that would suit you, wouldn't it? Wouldn't that suit you, if I collapsed on the way?"

"You won't collapse on the way, not you, Gran. If I know you, you'll stop at some café and fill your kite."

Mrs. McMullen stared at her grand-daughter. Begod, if she had the power she would strike her dead this moment. God forgive her for the thought, but she would. But on second thoughts, perhaps not dead, but dumb. She would have her dumb, like her son, so that she could talk at her and watch her burning herself up with frustration. If there was anybody in this world she hated more than another, it was this flesh of her own flesh. But there was little or none of her in this madam; she was all Shaughnessy; from her toes to the top of her head, she was all Shaughnessy . . . Mike Shaughnessy.

Mrs. McMullen now passed her grand-daughter in silence. Her head held high, her body erect, she went out of the room and, unaided, down the dim stairs.

Mary Ann sat down and drooped her face into her hands for a moment. Why was it that her grannie could make her feel so bad, so wicked? She felt capable of saying the most dreadful things when her grannie started on her. And everything had been lovely for those few minutes, with Corny's great news. Well, she straightened up, she wasn't going to let the old cat dampen this day. No, she wasn't. When they found Rose Mary they would celebrate; in some way they would celebrate, even with only ham and steamed pudding.

"Come on," she said, rising and holding out her hand to David, who had been standing strangely still on the middle of the hearth rug. His stillness now got through to her, and she bent to him swiftly, saying, "It's all right. It's all right. Rose Mary's only hiding. Come on, we'll find her."

Ten minutes later, with David still by the hand, she was standing on the drive-way when Corny brought the car back, and she looked at him, and he looked at her and shook his head. And it was a moment before he said, "Not a sign of her anywhere. I . . . I met the old girl half-way down the road and gave her a lift to the bus. She's black in the face with temper. You go for her?"

"Me go for her? You should have heard what she said. But don't bother about her, what's happened to Rose Mary?"

"You tell me. Why did she run out?"

"Because me grannie was at her an' all. She was saying . . . Oh. . . ." She put her fingers to her lips. "I know where she is." She pressed her head back into her shoulders as she stared at Corny. "She's gone to your grannie's."

"Me grannie's?"

"Yes, I bet that's where she's gone. That's how it started. Me grannie was needling her, and I heard her say she liked her Great-gran McBride, and me grannie said did she like her house and the smell an' all? Then Rose Mary said she didn't like her, and she ran out."

"But how would she get there, all that way?"

"She'd go on the bus, of course; she knows her way."

"Had she any money?"

"She could have taken it out of her pig, the bottom's loose."

"Well, did she?"

"I don't know, Corny; I haven't looked." Mary Ann's voice was high now, and agitated.

"Well, we'd better look, hadn't we?" He dashed from her and up the stairs, and when Mary Ann caught up with him he had the pig in his hand and the bottom was intact.

"She might have had some coppers in her pocket," Mary Ann said as she stared down at the pig. Then she added, "Oh, why had this to happen on such a day, too? Oh, Corny, suppose she's not at your grannie's."

He gripped her hand. "She's bound to be there. Look, I'll slip down; it won't take long. If she went by bus she'd just be there by now."

"Roo Marry!"

The scream startled them both. Then it came again "Roo Marry!" Not Romary but two distinct words now, Roo Marry.

They flew down the stairs, and there stood David on the drive, his body stiff, his mouth wide, ejecting the two words "Roo Marry!"

Corny hoisted him up into his arms, saying, "All right, all right. It's all right, David. Rose Mary will soon be here."

"Roo Marry! Roo Marry!"

Corny turned his strained face towards Mary Ann. "Rose Mary. He's saying Rose Mary."

"Yes, yes." She put her hands up to her son's face and cupped it, saying, "Don't cry, David. Don't cry. Rose Mary's only gone for a walk."

"Roo Marry! Roo Marry!" Now there followed some syllables in quick succession, unintelligible. Then again "Roo Marry!"

"Put him down and get to your grannie's."

Corny put David down, and Mary Ann took hold of the child's hand. Then, as Corny strode towards the car, he was stopped in his stride by a yell that said "Da-ad! Da-ad!" And he turned to see his son tugging his hand from Mary Ann's and stretching out his arm to him. Retracing his steps, he took the child's outstretched hand, saying, "I'll take him with me."

Long after the car had disappeared from her view, Mary Ann stood on the drive. She was possessed of a strange feeling, as

85

if she had lost everybody belonging to her. David had wanted to go with his dad. And he had said dad. In his own way he had said dad. He was talking. The wonder of it did not touch her in this moment, because Rose Mary was lost, really lost. . . . Don't be silly. She actually shook herself, and swung round and went into the house. But in a moment she was downstairs again and sitting in the office with the phone in her hand.

It was Mike who answered her. "Hello there," he said.

"It's me, Da. Tell me. Has Rose Mary come over there?"

"Rose Mary?" She could almost see her father's puckered brows. "No. What's happened?"

"Oh, so much, I don't know where to begin. Only we can't find Rose Mary. Corny's gone down to Gran McBride's. You see, me grannie came this morning. . . ."

"Oh, my God!"

"Yes, as you say, oh, my God! She was in fine fettle, and she taunted Rose Mary about something, and Rose Mary told her she didn't like her and she liked Grannie McBride, and then she ran out, and we think she may have made her way down there."

"God above! What mischief will that bloody woman cause next? Somebody should shoot her. Look, I'll come over. Have you looked everywhere round the place?"

"Yes, Da, we've looked everywhere. And don't come over yet; wait until Corny comes back. I'll ring you then; he might have found her."

"But what if he doesn't? What will you do then?"

"I don't know."

"Now look. If when Corny comes back he hasn't got her, you get on to the police straight-away."

"The police! But she might just be round about. . . ."

"Listen to me, girl. If Corny hasn't got her, get on to the police, and don't waste a minute. Look, I think I'll come over."

"All right, Da."

Mary Ann rang off, then sat looking out of the window to the side of her. This should have been a wonderful day, a marvellous day, but her grannie had to turn up, that evil genie, her grannie. Corny had made it at last; they should be rejoicing. And look what had happened. But she didn't really care about anything, about the garage, or the factory, or anything . . . if only Rose Mary would come back.

"Would you like a cigarette, Mrs. Boyle?" Jimmy was standing in the doorway, a grubby packet extended in his hand, and, shaking her head, she said softly, "No thanks, Jimmy."

"She'll turn up, never you fear, Mrs. Boyle. She's cute, and she's got a tongue in her head all right."

"Yes, Jimmy, she's got a tongue in her head. And she'll talk to anyone. That's what I'm afraid of." It had come upon her suddenly, this fear; as she had said to Jimmy, she'd talk to anyone. Oh, my God! She got off the seat and pushed past Jimmy; she wanted air. You heard of such dreadful things happening. That child, just a few months ago, taken away by that dreadful man. Oh, God in Heaven! Holy Mary, Mother of God, pray for us sinners now and at the hour of our death. Amen. Protect her. Oh, please, please. It won't matter about the garage, or money or anything, only protect her. . . . Here she was back to her childhood again, bargaining with the denizens of heaven. It was ridiculous, ridiculous. God helped those who helped themselves. She had learned that. . . . She must do something, but what? She had got to stay here until Corny returned. And then her da might come any minute. But she just couldn't stand about. She turned swiftly to Jimmy, saying, "I'm going up the road, to the crossroads. Tell Mr. Boyle if he comes back, I won't be long."

She was gone about twenty minutes, and when she returned there was the car on the drive and Corny standing at the office door with David by his side. Some part of her mind registered the fact in this moment that her son didn't rush to her, and she was hurt. The secret core in her was already crying. She stood in front of Corny and again he shook his head, then said, "She's never seen hilt nor hair of her, and I've stopped the car about twenty times and asked here and there."

"I phoned the farm; me da's coming over."

"I phoned an' all, from Jarrow."

Corny, his face bleached-looking, turned from her and went into the office and picked up the phone, and coming on his heels, she stood close to him and whispered, "What are you going to do?"

87

"Phone the police."

A few minutes later he put the phone down, saying, "They'll be here shortly." Then, rubbing his hand over his drained face, he walked out on to the drive, and he looked about him before he said, "I didn't think about it at the time when I was taking her to the bus, but now I wonder why I didn't throttle that old girl. Somebody's going to one of these days. I never really understood how you felt about her." He looked down at Mary Ann. "But I do now. My God! I do now."

8

The search was organised; the police cars were roaming the district. Mary Ann was walking the streets of Felling; Michael was doing Jarrow; Jimmy was stopping odd cars on the main road to enquire if anyone had seen a little girl in a blue dress, while Corny traversed the fields and ditches, and the by-lanes right to the old stone quarry four miles away and back to the garage, all the while humping David with him. As he came at a trot into the driveway carrying David on one arm, he heard the phone ring, but when he reached the office and lifted up the receiver the operator asked for his number.

He went out on to the drive again, David still by his side, and rubbed his sweating face with his hand. Where was Mike? Mike was supposed to stay put. "Mike!" he called. "Mike!" Then, going round to the back, he saw Mike's unmistakable figure in the far distance walking by the side of the deep drain.

Corny shook his head; they had done all that. He should have stayed here and waited for the phone. He had asked him to do just that because Jimmy was better on the road, and he himself was quicker on his pins over the fields, even handicapped as he was with the child. "Mike!" he shouted. "Mike!"

Mike was breathing hard when he reached the old car, and he called from there, "You've got news?"

Corny shook his head, and Mike's pace slowed.

"The phone's been ringing," said Corny when Mike reached him.

"Oh! Oh well, I was about for ages, I just couldn't stay put, man. I thought of the ditch over there. It's covered with ferns in places."

"We've been all round there, I've told you." Corny turned away and Mike's chin went upwards at the tone of his voice,

89

and then he lowered it again. This wasn't the time to take umbrage at a man's tone, not the state he must be in. For himself he was back to the time when Mary Ann had run away from the convent in the south and had been reported seen in the company of an old man. Those hours had nearly driven him to complete madness.

Around to the front of the garage again they went, David still hanging on to his father's hand. There, Corny stood, leaning for a moment against the wall. He felt exhausted both in mind and body; too much had happened too quickly in the last few hours. He couldn't ever remember feeling like this in his life before, weak, trembling all over inside.

"Da-ad."

David repeated the word and tugged twice at Corny's hand, before Corny looked at him, saying, "Yes. Yes, what is it, David?"

"Roo Marry . . . Lost?" The word lost was quite distinct.

Corny continued to look at his son for a moment. Then, lifting his eyes to Mike, he said, wearily, "I've always said part them and he'd talk. But God, I'd rather he remained dumb for life than this had to happen before he did it."

Mike said nothing but looked down at his grandson, to the little face swollen with crying. Lizzie, like Corny, had always maintained that the boy would talk if he hadn't Rose Mary to do it for him, and they had been right. He could talk all right, stumbling as yet, but, nevertheless, he had been shocked into speech.

Corny, now pulling himself from the wall, said, "If only that damned old witch hadn't put in an appearance this morning. With the news Mr. Blenkinsop brought me I should be on top of the world. I was for about five minutes."

"You will be again," said Mike. "Never you fear."

"That depends." Corny looked his father-in-law straight in the eye.

Again Mike made no answer, but he thought, "Aye, that depends."

Corny slowly moved towards the office with David at his side, and Mike, walking on his other side, looked towards the ground as he said, "I don't think there's a woman anywhere who's caused as much havoc as that one. You know . . . and this is the truth . . . twice . . . twice I've thought seriously of doing her in." He turned his head to the side and met Corny's full gaze. "It's a fact. When I think, and I've often thought that I could have been hung for her, I get frightened, but not like I used to, because she can't make me rise now as she could a few years ago. And I'm positive that's why she came here to-day, just to get Mary Ann on the raw, because when she came to us on Sunday she got no satisfaction. Peter was at the tea-table, and Peter in his polite, gentlemanly way is a match for her. And we were all laughing our heads off and not taking a pennorth of notice of her. She didn't like it. She couldn't make anybody rise. Everybody was too happy for her. But she couldn't go a week without finding a target, so she came back to the old firm. Who better than her grand-daughter? God, I wish she had dropped down dead on the way."

"I endorse that. By, I do!" Corny shook his head. Then, drawing in a deep breath and looking down at David, he said, "Are you hungry?"

"NO-t."

"You're not hungry?"

"No-t, Da-ad."

"Would you like some milk?"

"No-t."

"Say, no, David."

"No-oo."

"That's a good boy." Corny turned and looked at Mike, and their glances said, "Would you believe it?"

Now David, crossing his legs, pulled at Corny's hand and said quite distinctly, "Lav, Da-ad."

"Well, you know where it is, don't you? You can go by yourself. . . . Go on."

David went, and as Corny and Mike watched him running round the corner of the building, the phone rang. Within a second Corny was in the office and had the receiver to his ear. "Yes?"

"Mr. Boyle?"

"Yes, Mr. Boyle here."

"It's Blenkinsop."

"Oh, hello, Mr. Blenkinsop."

"I don't know how to begin, for I suppose you're nearly all mad at that end. . . . You'd never believe it, but . . . but I've got her here."

Corny closed his eyes and, gripping Mike's arm tightly, he wetted his lips, then said, "You did say you've got her there, Mr. Blenkinsop?"

"Yes. Yes, I've got her here all right. She gave me the shock of my life. I stopped at an hotel for a drink and when I came out, there she was, sitting as calm as you like in the front of the car."

"In the front of the car?" Corny repeated slowly as he cast his eyes towards Mike. "How did she get there?"

"Well, as far as I can gather she was hiding from someone, great-grandmother or someone, so she says, and she climbed into the boot, as the lid was partly open. At this moment I feel I should pray to somebody in thanks that the lid was open and wouldn't close tight because of some gear I had in there. She says she fell asleep because it was hot, but woke up once the car got going and did a lot of knocking, and, by the look of her face, a lot of crying, and then she fell asleep again. Apparently she found no difficulty in lifting the lid up once the car had stopped. One thing I can't understand and that is how she slept in there at all, especially when the car was moving."

"Oh, she's been used to sleeping on journeys since she was a baby. They both have, her and David."

"Well, boy, am I dazed. But you . . . you must be frantic."

"You can say that again. The whole place is alerted. The police, the lot. But I never thought of you, not once."

"Well, who would? I tell you, she gave me a scare sitting there; I thought I was seeing things. Look. Here she is; have a word with her."

Corny bowed his head and closed his eyes and listened.

"It's me, Dad."

"Hello, Rose Mary." His voice was trembling.

"I didn't mean to do it, Dad, but I wanted to hide from Great-gran. I didn't want to go back upstairs, 'cos she was horrible, and so I climbed into the boot, like it was the old car. The lid was open a bit but it was hot. When the car started going I tried to push the lid up, and I shouted, but it was noisy. Are you all right, Dad?"

"Yes, yes, I'm all right, Rose Mary. We only wondered where you were."

"And David? Is he wanting me?"

"David's all right, too."

"And me ma. Did she cry?"

"Yes, yes, because she couldn't find you, but she'll be all right now."

"I'm sorry, Dad."

"It's all right. It's all right, Rose Mary."

"Mr. Blenkinsop has been trying to get on the phone a lot."

"Has he? We've been out and about."

"I'm going to have some dinner now and then I'm coming back. . . . You're not mad at me, Dad, are you?"

"No, no, I'm not mad at you."

"You sound funny."

"And so do you."

He heard her give a little laugh. Then he said, "Let me speak to Mr. Blenkinsop again."

"Ta-rah, Dad."

"Bye-bye, Rose Mary."

"Well now." It was Mr. Blenkinsop speaking again. "If it's all right with you, as she says she'll have some dinner, and then I'll make the return journey as quickly as possible."

"I'm sorry, sir, if this has spoiled your trip."

"Oh, don't be sorry about that. I'm sorry for scaring the day-lights out of you. And if I know anything you're still in a state of shock; I know how I would feel. . . . I tell you what though. We're just about twenty miles out of Doncaster; I wonder if you'd mind if I ran in and told my cousin . . . I was going to spend the night with him and his family—I think I told you—and if I explain things they'll understand, because I won't make the return journey back to them until to-morrow."

"Yes, yes, you go ahead and do that. I'm sorry it's putting you out."

"Oh, not at all. Just that being so near, it would be better to explain in person, rather than phoning."

Mr. Blenkinsop laughed his merry laugh. "What a day! What a day! I'm just thinking; I brought you a bit of good news and then I took all the good out of it."

"It wasn't your fault, sir."

"Well, I'm glad you look at it like that. I'll be back as quickly as I can, and that should be shortly after six."

"Right, sir."

"Here she is to say another good-bye."

Corny heard Rose Mary take a number of sharp breaths. "Bye-bye again, Dad. Tell David I won't be long. And me mam."

"Bye-bye, dear."

He listened until the receiver clicked, then put the phone down and turned and looked at Mike. Mike was leaning against the stanchion of the door, wiping his face and neck with a coloured handkerchief. Corny sat staring at him. He felt very weak as if he had just got over a bout of flu or some such thing.

"Well!" said Mike, still rubbing at his face.

"Aye, well," said Corny. "I just can't take it in. I feel so sick with relief I could vomit."

The corner of Mike's mouth turned up as he said, "Well, before you give yourself that pleasure you'd better get on to the police."

"Aye, yes." Corny picked up the phone again.

"Aw, I'm glad to hear that," said the officer-in-charge. "Right glad."

"I'm sorry to have put you to so much trouble."

"Oh, don't bother about that. As long as she's O.K., that's everything. I'll start calling them off now."

"Thank you very much. Good-bye."

Corny walked past Mike and looked up at the sky. He still felt bewildered.

"What are you going to do now?"

"Go and find Mary Ann," said Corny. "She seemed to think she might have gone to some of her playmates. I'll go round

94

Felling, and when I pick her up I'll go and find Michael. That's if the police haven't contacted him beforehand. . . . You'll stay here?"

"Oh, aye, I'll stay here. I feel like yourself, a bit sick with relief."

"Da-ad be-en."

The two men turned to where David was running across the cement towards them, and when the boy threw himself against Corny's legs, Corny looked down at him but didn't speak, and Mike, after a moment, said softly, "Aren't you going to tell him?"

Corny looked at Mike now and he said slowly, "I've only got till six o'clock."

"What d'you mean?"

Corny, now speaking under his breath, muttered, "The minute she comes back he'll close up like a clam; she hasn't been away long enough."

"Aw man, my God, be thankful." Mike's voice was indignant.

"I am, I am, Mike. Thankful! You just don't know how thankful, but this"—he motioned his head down to the side of him—"I wanted to hear him. . . . You know what?" He moved his lips soundlessly. "More than anything in life I wanted to hear him. . . . I wanted this garage to be successful as you know. For seven years I've hung on, but if I had to choose, well, I know what I would have chosen. . . . His state has come between me and sleep for months now. I've told Mary Ann that if . . ." He looked down at David again, at the wide eyes staring up at him, and, looking back at Mike, he began to speak enigmatically, saying, "If what has happened the day could have been made to happen, you know what I mean, one one place, one the other, just for a short time, it would have worked. I've told her till I'm sick, but she wouldn't have it. But I've been proved right, haven't I? You see for yourself."

"Yes, I see. And Lizzie's always said the same thing. But be thankful, lad, be thankful. He won't close up."

"I wish I could bet on that. She'll be so full of talk that he'll just stand and gape."

"Ssh, man! Ssh!" Mike turned away with a jerk of his head

95

towards David, and Corny, now looking down at his son's strained face and trembling lips, said, "Rose Mary is coming back, David."

"Ro-se Ma-ry," the child's lips stretched wide, and then he again said, on a high note, "Ro-se Ma-ry." The name was clear-cut now.

"Yes, Rose Mary is coming back. You remember the American man, Mr. Blenkinsop?"

David nodded his head, and Corny repeated, "You remember the American man, Mr. Blenkinsop?"

"Ya."

"Yes," said Corny.

"Ye-as," said David.

"Well, Rose Mary was hiding in the boot of his car, and he drove away and she couldn't get out. . . . What do you think of that?"

The light in David's eyes deepened, his mouth stretched wider, and then he laughed.

"I'm going to pick up Mam now. Do you want to come?"

"Ye-as," said David.

"Go on, then, get into the car." Now Corny, turning to Mike, said, "If she should phone in tell her I'll wait outside the school. That's the best place."

"Good enough," said Mike. "Get yourself off."

Corny brought the car out of the garage and stopped it when he neared Mike, and, looking at David sitting on the seat beside him, he said, "Say good-bye to Granda."

"Bye, Gran . . . da."

"Good-bye, son."

Corny, with his face close to Mike, looked him in the eyes and said, softly, "You know, it's in me to wish that she wasn't coming back to-night or to-morrow."

"Corny! Corny, don't be like that!" Mike's voice was harsh.

"She's safe so I'm content. And I say again, give me another day, perhaps two, and I'd have no fears after that. But just you wait until to-night, it'll be a clam again, you'll see."

"Aw, go on now. Go on and stop thinking such nonsense." Mike stepped back and waved Corny away, and as he watched him driving into the road he thought, "That's a nice attitude to take! There'll be skull and hair flying if he talks like that to her." But after a moment of considering he turned in the direction of the office, asking himself what he would have felt like if Michael had, to all intents and purposes, been dumb? Pretty much like Corny was feeling now, because he knew, in a strange sort of way, that he and Corny were built on similar lines and that their reactions, in the main, were very much alike.

"Look, have a drop of brandy." Corny was on his hunkers before Mary Ann, where she sat in a straight-backed chair in the kitchen.

"No, I'm all right. I'm all right; it's just the reaction; it's just that I can't stop shaking."

"I'll get you a drop of brandy. . . . You keep it in as a medicine, and this is a time when medicine is needed." Corny went to the cupboard and, reaching to the back of the top shelf, brought out a half-bottle of brandy, and, pouring a measure into a cup, he took it to her. Placing it in her hand, he said gently, "There now, sup it up."

"I don't like brandy."

"It doesn't matter what you like, get it down you. Come on." He guided the cup to her lips, and when she sipped at it she shuddered. Then, looking at him, she said, "What time did he say he'd be back?"

"Something after six."

"And it's just on five." She raised her eyes to the clock. Then, stretching out her hand, she put the cup on the table near where David was standing looking out of the window, waiting for a glimpse of the car that would bring Rose Mary back, but the movement of her hand caught his attention and he turned from the window and, looking from the cup to Mary Ann, he said distinctly, "Sup?"

There was a quick exchange of glances between Corny and Mary Ann, and, smiling now, she said, "No, David, it's nasty." Then again she was looking at Corny, the smile gone, as she said, "I can't believe it. I just can't believe it. I won't be able to really take it in until I see her."

97

Corny made no answer to this. He was looking towards David, where the boy was again gazing out of the window, and he said softly, "I always told you, didn't I? Get them apart for a while. . . ."

"It wasn't that, it wasn't that." Mary Ann was on her feet. "It was the shock."

"Aye, you're right. But if she had come back right away there would have been no chit-chat, not like now. . . . As it is, I'm a bit afraid that as soon as she puts her face in the door he'll close. . . ."

At this moment they heard a knocking on the staircase door and Jimmy's voice calling, "The phone's going, boss. You're wanted on the phone."

As Corny made swiftly for the door Mary Ann was on his heels, and she was still close behind him when he entered the office, and when, with his hand on the phone, he turned and looked at her, he said quietly, "It's all right, it's all right, there's nothing to worry about now."

She shook her head as she watched him lift the phone to his ear. "Hello. Oh, it's you, Mr. Blenkinsop. Hello there, every-thing all right?" Although he wasn't looking at Mary Ann he felt her body stiffen, and when Mr. Blenkinsop's voice came to him, saying, "Oh yes, as right as rain," he cast a quick glance at her and smiled reassuringly, then listened to Mr. Blenkinsop going on, "It's just that I thought I'd better phone you as I've not been able to get away from my cousin's yet. You see he has four sons and there was quite a drought of female company around her, and they've got her now up in the train-room. I've had two unsuccessful attempts at getting her away; not that she seems very eager to leave them. They've gone right overboard for her. Their verdict is she's cute. This is quite unanimous, from Ian who is three, to Donald who is ten. So, as it is, it's going to be nearer nine when I arrive . . . I hope you're not mad."

"No, Mr. Blenkinsop. That's O.K., as long as she's all right."

"All right? I'll say she's all right. Can you hear that hulla-baloo?" He stopped speaking, and Corny hadn't to strain his ears to hear the excited shrieks and the sound of running feet. Then Mr. Blenkinsop's voice came again, saying, "They've just come in like a herd of buffalo."

Corny turned his eyes to Mary Ann again. There was an anxious look on her face, but he smiled at her and wrinkled his nose before turning his attention to the phone again as Mr. Blenkinsop's voice said, "Just a minute. There's a conclave going on, they want to ask you something. Just a minute, will you?"

As Corny waited he put his hand over the mouthpiece and said under his breath, "She's having the time of her life."

"He hasn't left there yet?"

"No, there's four children, boys, and apparently they've got a train set. They're kicking up a racket." As he looked at her strained face he said, "It's all right, it's all right, there's nothing to worry about."

"Hello. Yes . . . yes, I'm here."

"Look, I don't know how to put this but they're all around me here, the four of them . . . and their mother and the father an' all. Well . . . well, it's like this, they want me to say will you let Rose Mary stay the night?"

". . . Stay the night?" Corny put his hand out quickly to stop Mary Ann grabbing the phone, and he shook his head vigorously at her and pressed the receiver closer to his ear to hear Mr. Blenkinsop say, "You know, if you could agree to this it would save me a return journey to-morrow because Dave, my cousin here, and me, well we could get through our business to-night and I'd make an early start in the morning. But that's up to you. I know that you and your lady are bound to want her back, but there it is." There was a pause which Corny did not fill, and then Mr. Blenkinsop's voice came again, saying, "Would you like to speak to her? Here she is."

"Hello, Dad."

"Hello, Rose Mary. Are you all right?"

"Oh yes, Dad. It's lovely here. They've got a big house and garden, an' a train-room, and they're all boys." Her next words were drowned in the high laughter of children.

"Don't you want to come back to David?" As Corny listened

to her answer he held out his free arm, stiffly holding Mary Ann at a distance from the phone.

"Oh yes, Dad. Yes, I wish David was here. And you, and me mam. Is me mam all right?"

"Yes, she's fine. And would you like to stay there until the morrow?"

"No! no!" Mary Ann's voice hissed at him as he heard Rose Mary say, "Yes, Dad, if it's all right with you and me mam."

"Yes, it's all right with us, dear. You have a good time and enjoy yourself, and then you can tell us all about it to-morrow. Well, good-bye now."

"Bye-bye, Dad. Bye-bye."

As Mary Ann rushed out of the office he listened to Mr. Blenkinsop saying, "We'll take great care of her. She's made a great impression here. I think you'd better prepare yourself for the visit of four stalwart youths in the future."

Corny gave a weak laugh, then said, "Well, until to-morrow morning, Mr. Blenkinsop."

"Yes, until to-morrow morning. I'll bring her back safe and sound, never fear. Good-bye now."

"Good-bye." Corny put down the phone and tried to tell himself that he was disappointed that she wasn't coming back to-night. And then Mary Ann appeared in the doorway again.

"You shouldn't have done it."

"What could I have done?"

"You could have told him that I was nearly out of my mind and I wanted her back."

"Well, she's coming back. It's only a few more hours, and the man asked me as a favour."

"Oh yes, you'd have to grant him a favour, knowing how I felt, knowing that I was waiting every minute. You know. . . ." She strained her face up to him. "You're glad, aren't you, you're glad that she's not coming back to-night because it'll keep them apart a little longer. You're glad."

"Now don't go on like that. Don't be silly."

"I'm not being silly. I know what's in your mind; you've been preening yourself, ever since I got in, about him talking, that it would never have happened if they hadn't been separated.

You were frightened of her coming back in case he wouldn't keep up the effort."

"All right, all right." He was shouting now. "Yes I was, and I still am. And yes, I'm glad that she's not coming back until to-morrow morning. It'll give him a chance, for he damn well hadn't a chance before. She not only talked for him, she thought for him, and lived for him; she lived his life, he hadn't any of his own. . . . I'll tell you this. He's been a new being this afternoon. And I'll tell you something else, I wish they had invited her for a week."

There was a long, long silence, during which they stared at each other. Then Mary Ann, her voice low and bitter, said, "I hate you. Oh, how I hate you!" Then she turned slowly from him, leaving him leaning against the little desk, his head back, his eyes closed, his teeth grating the skin on his lip.

I hate you! Mary Ann had said that to him. Oh, how I hate you!

"Da-ad." Corny opened his eyes and looked down to where David was standing in the open doorway, his face troubled, and he said, "Yes, son. What is it?"

"Ma-am." There followed a pause before David, his mouth wide open now, emitted the word, "Cry."

Corny considered his son. The child had seen his mother cry, yet he hadn't gone to her, he had come to him. He reached out and took his hand. Then, hoisting him up on to the desk, he looked straight at him as he said, "Mam's crying because Rose Mary is not coming back until to-morrow."

David's eyes remained unblinking.

"You're not going to cry because Rose Mary isn't coming back until to-morrow, are you?"

The eyes still unblinking, the expression didn't change, and then David slowly shook his head.

"Say, No, Dad."

"No, Da-ad."

"That's a good boy. I'm going to mend a car. Are you coming to help me?"

Again David moved his head, nodding now, and again Corny prompted him. "Say, Yes, Dad."

"Yes, Da-ad."

"Come on then." He lifted him down, and they walked out of the office side by side and into the garage, and as he went Corny thought, "I'll give her a little while to cool off and then I'll go up."

9

If Corny hadn't heard the car slow up and thought it was someone wanting petrol he would never have gone on to the drive at that moment and seen her going.

The occupants of the car decided not to stop after all, and it was speeding away to the right of the garage. But, going down the road to the left, Corny stared at the back of Mary Ann. Mary Ann carrying a case. He stood petrified for a moment, one hand raised in mid-air in an appealing gesture. God Almighty! She wouldn't. No, she wouldn't do that without saying a word. She was near the bend of the road when he sprang forward and yelled, "Mary Ann!" When there was no pause in her step he stopped at the end of the line of white bricks edging the roadway, and now, his voice high and angry, he yelled, "Do you hear? Mary Ann!"

Taking great loping strides, he raced towards her, and again he shouted, "Mary Ann! Wait a minute, Mary Ann!" It wasn't until he saw her hasten her step that he stopped again, and after a moment of grim silence he yelled, "If you go, you go. Only remember this. You come back on your own, I'll not fetch you. I'm telling you." Her step didn't falter, and the next minute she was lost to his sight round the bend.

The anger seeped out of him. He felt as if his life was seeping out of him, draining down from his veins into the ground. How long he stood still he didn't know, and he wasn't conscious of turning about and walking back to the garage. He didn't come to himself until he saw David standing with his back to the petrol pump. She hadn't even come to see the child. She was bats about the boy, she was bats about them both. Why hadn't she taken him with her? Perhaps because she knew that he wouldn't have let him go. And she was right there. He wouldn't have let the boy go with her.

"Ma-am. . . ."

Corny looked down at the small, trembling lips, and he forced himself to speak calmly, saying, "Mam's gone to Gran's."

"Gra-an's?"

"Your Grannie Shaughnessy has got a bad head, she's not very well. Can you go upstairs and set the tray for your supper, do you think? Your Bunny tray with the mug and the plate. Then wash yourself."

The boy was looking up at him, his eyes wide and deep, with that knowing look in their depths. Then he said, "Yes, Da-ad," and went slowly towards the house. And Corny turned about and went into the office and dropped into his chair. He felt weak again and, something more, he felt frightened; this kind of thing happened to other fellows, to other couples, but it couldn't happen to them. He had loved her since he was a boy, and she had loved him from when she was ten. She had loved and championed him since he could remember. She had stood by him through all the hard times. And there had been hard times; there had been weeks when they both had to pull their belts in in order that their children got their full share of food, and during these times both had resisted gobbling up food when they went to the farm on a Sunday and sat down to the laden table. No one must know how things really stood. They would get by. It was she who had always said that. "We'll get by," she'd said. "We'll have a break, you'll see. It'll come. . . ." And it had come; it had come to-day, like a bolt from the blue. And with it the break in his family had come too.

But it just couldn't happen to him and Mary Ann. They had made a pact at the beginning, never to go to sleep on a row, and they never had. Well, there was always a first time, and by the looks of things that first time was now, because she had no intention of coming back to-day; she had taken a case with her. He dropped his head on to his hands. And all because he hadn't said the word that would bring Rose Mary back to-night. What were a few more hours of separation if it was going to loosen her son's tongue? Couldn't she see it? No; because she didn't want to see it. She didn't want them separated for a minute from each other, or from her. She had once said they were as close as the Blessed Trinity, and on that occasion he had asked where he came in in the divine scheme of things, and she had laughingly replied, "We'll make you Joseph." But he was no Joseph, he was no foster-father. David was his son, and he had carried a deep secret ache, a yearning to hear his voice. And now he was hearing it, but he was going to pay dearly apparently for that pleasure.

He heard a car come on to the drive and it brought him to his feet, and when he reached the office door, there, scrambling out from a dilapidated Austin, was Jimmy and his pals. Corny had never seen this lot before. He had seen other pals of Jimmy's, but they hadn't been so freakish as the boys now confronting him. These looked like a combination of The Rolling Stones and The Pretty Things, and Jimmy looked the odd man out, because he appeared the only male thing among them. At any other time Corny would have hooted inside, he would have chipped this lot and stood being chipped in return, but not to-night. His face was straight as he looked at Jimmy and asked, "Well?"

"I just popped in, Boss—we was passing like—just to see if Rose Mary was back."

"No, she's not back. She's staying with Mr. Blenkinsop's friends until the morning. He's bringing her back then."

"Oh." Jimmy now turned and nodded towards his four long-haired companions, who were all surveying Corny with a blank, scrutinising stare.

"The missus all right?" Jimmy glanced up at the house-window as he spoke, and Corny, after a moment, said, "Yes. Yes, she's all right."

"Busy, is she?"

"No." Corny screwed up his eyes in enquiry. "She's got a headache; she's lying down. Do you want something?"

"No, no, boss. I was just wondering, after all the excitement of the day, how she was farin'. And we was just passing like I said. Well, fellas," he turned towards the four, "let's get crackin'."

The four boys piled back into the car. Not one of them had spoken, but Jimmy, now taking his seat beside the driver, put his hand out of the window and passed it over the rust-encrusted chrome framing the door and, smiling broadly, said, "She goes."

"You're lucky." Corny nodded to him but did not grin, as he would have done at another time when making a scathing remark, even if it was justified, and Jimmy's long face lengthened even further, his mouth dropped, and his eyebrows twitched. He sensed there was something not quite right. The boss was off-hand, summat was up. "Be seeing you the mornin'," he said.

For answer, Corny merely nodded his head, and as the car swung out of the driveway he went into the office. . . .

Again he was sitting with his head in his hands when the phone rang. He stared at it for a moment. He knew who it would be . . . Mike. Slowly he reached out and, lifting up the receiver, said, "Yes."

"Corny."

He had been wrong; it wasn't her da, it was her ma. Lizzie's voice sounded very low, as if she didn't want to be overheard. "I'm sorry about this, Corny."

He didn't speak. What was there to say?

"Are you there?"

"Yes, I'm here, Mam."

"I want you to know that I'm with you in this."

He widened his eyes at the phone.

"I've always said if they were separated, even for a short time, it would give him a chance. I've told her I think you're right. But . . . but, on the other hand, she's been worried nearly out of her mind and it mightn't have been the right time to have done it."

"What other chance would I have had? You tell me."

"I don't know, but, as I said, I'm with you. I can't tell her that, you understand, not at present. She's in an awful state, Corny. . . . What are you going to do?"

"Me?"

"Yes, you. Who else?"

"I'm going to do nothing, Mam. She walked out on me, she didn't even come and see the boy. I ran down the road after her, yelling me head off, but she wouldn't stop. I wouldn't even have known she had gone, it was just by chance I saw her. So what am I going to do? I'm going to do nothing."

"Oh dear. Corny. Corny. You know what she is; she's as stubborn as a mule."

"Well, there's more than one mule."

"That's going to get neither of you anywhere. And you've got to think of the children."

"It strikes me you can think of the children too much. In one way I mean. The children shouldn't come before each other. Whatever has got to be done with the children should be a combined effort."

"Well, you didn't make it much of a combined effort from what I hear, Corny. You told that man that Rose Mary could stay until to-morrow morning, and didn't give her the chance to say a word."

"Well, what harm was there in it? Just a few more hours. And if she had been unhappy then I would have whisked her back like a shot; I would have gone out there for her myself; but by the sound of her she was having the time of her life. And at this end David wasn't worrying. That is what really upset madam, David wasn't really worrying. What was more, he was talking."

"He'll worry if she doesn't come back soon. . . . I mean Mary Ann not Rose Mary."

"I think he's worrying already, he's trying not to cry." Corny's voice was flat now.

"Would Mike come over and get him?"

"No, Mam, no thank you." His voice was no longer flat. "The boy stays with me. If she wants him she's got to come back home. . . . Home I said, Mam. This is her home, Mam."

"I know that, I know that well enough, Corny. And don't shout."

"Where is she?"

"She's gone down to the bottom field to see Mike."

There followed a short silence. And then Lizzie spoke again, saying, "It seems terrible for this to happen, and on a day when you've got such wonderful news."

"Oh, she told you that, did she?"

"Yes, she told me. I'm so glad, Corny, I'm delighted for you. If only this business was cleared up."

"Well, there's a way to end it. She knows what to do. She walked down the road, she can walk up it again."

"Don't be so stubborn, Corny. Get in the car and come over."

"Not on your life."

"Very well, there's no use talking any more, is there?" Lizzie's voice was cut off abruptly, and Corny, taking the phone from his ear, stared at it for a moment before putting it on the stand.

Go over there. Beg her to come back. Say he was sorry. For what? For acting rationally, sensibly?

He marched upstairs and into the kitchen. David had put his mug and plate on the tray but was now standing looking out of the window. He turned an eager face to Corny on his entry, then looked towards the table and the tray, and Corny said, "By, that's clever of you! Are you hungry?"

David nodded his head; then before Corny had time to prompt him, he said, "Yes, Da-ad."

"You'd like some cheese, wouldn't you?"

David now grinned at him and nodded as he said, "Yes, Da-ad, cheese." He thrust his lips out on the word and Corny was forced to smile. Cheese upset his stomach; it brought him out in a rash; but that was before he could say cheese. He would see what effect it had on him now.

He was cutting a thin slice of cheese from the three-cornered piece when he heard the distant tinkle of the phone ringing again. "You eat that," he said quickly, placing the cheese on a piece of bread. Then he patted David on the head and hurried out.

This time it was Mike on the phone, and without any preamble he began, "Now what in the name of God is all this about? What do you think the pair of you are up to?"

Corny, staring out of the little office-window, passed his teeth tightly over each other before saying, with forced calmness, "Well, I'm glad you said the pair of us and didn't just put the lot on me."

"That's as it may be." Mike's voice was rough. "But this I'm going to say to you, and you alone. What the hell were you at to let her come away?"

"Now look you here, Mike. I don't happen to have sentries posted at each corner of the house to let me know her movements; I didn't even know she was going until I saw the back of her going down the road. . . ."

"Well, why didn't you bring her back?"

"Look, I shouted and shouted to her, and the harder I shouted the quicker she walked."

"You had legs, hadn't you? You could have run after her."

There was a long pause following this. Then Corny, his voice low, very low now, said, "Yes, I had legs, and I could have run. And I could have picked her up bodily and carried her back. That's what you mean, isn't it? Well, now, you put yourself in my position, Mike. Liz walks out on you; you run after her; you call to her, and she takes not a damned bit of notice of you. What would you have done? She's got a case in her hand; she's leaving you and her son . . . and, this is the point, Mike, she's going home."

"Oh, I get your point all right. But what do you mean, home? That's her home."

"Aye, it should be, but she's never looked on this as home; she's always looked on your place, the farm, as home. And there she was, case in hand . . . going home. Think a minute. What would you have done, eh?"

"Well." Mike's voice faltered now. "Most girls look upon their parents' place as home. Look at Michael here. Never away, even when he's finished work. That's nothing."

"It mightn't be nothing to you, but it's something to me. She knew what she was taking on when she married me. This was the only home I could give her until I could get a better, and now, when the prospects of doing just that are looking large, this happens."

"You're a pair of hot-headed fools." Mike's voice was calmer now. "Look, get into the car and come over."

"No, not on your life, Mike. If there's any coming over she's going to do it. She can get cool in the stew she got hot in."

"Man!" Mike's voice was rising again. "She's upset. More than upset, she looks awful. You know for a fact yourself she just lives for those bairns."

"Yes," shouted Corny now. "I know for a fact she just lives for those bairns. She's lived for them so much she's almost forgotten that I've got a share in them. If she'd done what I'd asked months ago and let you have David for a few days this would never have happened. But no. No, she couldn't bear either of them out of her sight. She made on it was because she didn't want them separated, they mustn't be separated, but the real truth of the matter is that she couldn't bear to let one of them go, not even for a night. All this could have been avoided if she had acted sensibly."

"It's all right saying if . . . if . . . the thing's done. But you can't stick all the blame for what's happened to-day on her. The one to blame is that blasted old she-devil. If she hadn't come along Rose Mary would have been home this minute and nothing like this would have happened. The trouble that old bitch causes stuns me when I think about it."

There was silence again between them. Then Mike's voice, coming very low, with a plea in it, said, "When you shut up the garage come on over. Come on, man. Drop in as if nothing had happened."

Slowly Corny put the receiver back on to its stand. Then looking at it, he muttered, "Aw no, Mike. Aw no. You don't get me going crawling, not in this way, you don't. I've just to start that and I'm finished."

10

Mary Ann stood at the window of the room that had been hers from a child. She had never thought she would spend a night here again, at least not alone, unless something had happened to Corny. Well, something had happened to Corny.

She stood with her arms crossed over her breast, her hands on her shoulders, hugging herself in her misery. There was a moon shining somewhere. The light was picking out the farm buildings; the whole landscape looked peaceful, and beautiful, but she did not feel the peace, nor see the beauty. She was looking back to the eternity that she had lived through, from the minute she had come back home yesterday.

She had never for a moment thought that he would let her go. Although she had been flaming with temper against him, the sensible, reasonable part of her was waiting for him to convince her that he was right. When she heard his voice calling to her along the road she had felt a wave of relief pass over her; she wouldn't have to go through with it. He would come dashing up and grip her by the shoulders and shake her, and go for her hell for leather. He would say, "Did you mean what you said about hating me?" And after a time she would say, "How could I? How could I ever hate you, whatever you did?"

All this had been going on in the reasonable, sensible part of her, but on the surface she was still seething, still going to show him. After he had called her name for a second time and she heard his footsteps pounding along the road behind her she quickened her stride and told herself she wasn't going to make this easy for him. Then she was near the bend and his footsteps stopped, and his voice came to her again, saying, "If you go, you go. Only remember this, you come back on your own, I'll not fetch you." That forced her pride up and she couldn't stop walking, not even when she was round the bend, although her step was much slower.

When she was on the bus she just couldn't believe that she was doing this thing, that she was walking out on him, walking out on David. But David wasn't hers any more, he was his. He had claimed David as something apart from Rose Mary.

Her temper had disappeared and she was almost in a state of collapse when she reached the farm. The shock of Rose Mary's disappearance was telling in full force and it had been some time before she had given her mother a coherent picture of what had happened. And then, later, she was further bemused and hurt when Lizzie, of all people, took Corny's side in the matter, because her mother had always had reservations about Corny, but in this case she seemed wholeheartedly for him.

It was only her da's reactions that had soothed her. He didn't blame her, he understood. After talking to Corny on the phone he had put his arm about her and said, "Don't you worry, he'll be along later," and she hadn't answered, "I don't want him to come along later. I don't care if I never see him again," which would have been the expected reaction to a quarrel such as theirs. She had said nothing, she had just waited. She had waited, and waited, and when ten o'clock came, her mother had said, "Go to bed; things will clear themselves to-morrow."

The clock on the landing struck three. She wondered if he was asleep, or was he, too, looking out into the night. She remembered their pact, never to go to sleep on a quarrel. She had the urge to get dressed and fly across the fields, cutting the main roads, by-passing Felling, and running up the lane to the house and hammering on the door. But no, no, if she did that, that would be the end of her, he'd be top dog for life.

By eleven o'clock the following morning the bitterness was high in Mary Ann again. Her da, Michael, and her mother were in the kitchen. It was coffee time, and their Michael, forgetting that she was no longer an impulsive child but the mother of two six-year-old children, was leading off at her, "You know yourself you were always ram-stam, pell-mell, you never stopped to think. Now I know Corny as well as anybody, and if you're going to sit here waiting till he comes crawling back you're going to have corns on your backside."

"Oh, shut up, our Michael. What do you know about it?"

"I know this much. I think Corny's right. I also know that you haven't changed very much over the years. Oppose you in anything and whoof! The balloon goes up."

"That's enough," Mike said sharply, his hand raised. He looked towards Michael as he spoke and made a warning motion with his head.

During the heated conversation Lizzie had said nothing; she just sat sipping her coffee. And so it was she who first heard the car draw up in the roadway. This was nothing unusual, but the next moment a faint and high-pitched cry of "Mam! Mam!" brought her eyes wide, and her head turned to the others, and she cried to Mike, who was now consoling Mary Ann with the theory that Corny was waiting for Rose Mary to arrive and then he'd bring them both across, "Quiet a minute! Listen!" And as they listened there came the call again, nearer now, and the next minute the back door burst open and Rose Mary came flying through the scullery and into the kitchen, and as she threw herself at Mary Ann, Mike cried, "Well, what did I tell you? It was as I said." His face was beaming. Then breaking in on his grand-daughter's babbling, he cried, "Where's your dad? Has he gone on the farm?"

"Me dad?" Rose Mary turned her face over her shoulder. "No, Grandad; me dad's back home. Mr. Blenkinsop brought me. He's looking in the cow byres, waitin'."

Mary Ann rose to her feet, and, looking down at Rose Mary, she said quietly, "Mr. Blenkinsop? Why did he bring you here, not home?"

"Me dad asked him, Mam. He did take me home, and me dad said would he drop me over." Rose Mary now glanced about her quickly, and added, "Where's David? Where is he, Mam?"

"David?" There was a quick exchange of glances among the elders, and then Mary Ann said, "Didn't you see David when you went home?"

Rose Mary screwed up her face as she looked up at her mother, and her voice dropped to a low pitch when she said, "No, Mam.

David wasn't there. I just got out of the car and me dad said hello and . . . and kissed me; then he asked Mr. Blenkinsop to bring me over 'cos you were here, and I thought David was with you. . . . Isn't he, Mam?"

Mary Ann stood with her head back for a moment, looking over the heads of the others. Her fists were pressed between her breasts, trying to stop this new pain from going deep into the core of her. He had split them up, deliberately split them up, giving her Rose Mary and keeping David; he had not only split the twins, he had split her and him apart, he had rent the family in two. Oh God! She drooped her head slowly now as she heard Mike say, "I'd better go and see this man."

"No. . . . No, leave this to me." She walked stiffly towards the door, and when Rose Mary made to accompany her she said, "Stay with your grannie, I'll be with you in a minute."

She found the American, as she thought of him, talking to Jonesy in the middle of the yard. When she came up to them Jonesy moved away and she said, "Mr. Blenkinsop?"

"Yes, ma'am. Well." He moved his head from side to side. "I don't know how to start my apologies. You must have been worried stiff yesterday."

"Yes, yes I was, Mr. Blenkinsop."

"Well, she's back safe and sound and she's had the time of her life. She floored them all, they went overboard for her, hook, line, and sinker. . . ." His voice trailed away as he stared down at this pocket-sized young woman. There was something here he couldn't get straight. He was quick to sum people up; he had summed her husband up and found him an honest, straightforward young fellow, and also a man who had, you could say, taken to him, but she was a different kettle of fish. She wasn't for him in some ways. The antipathy came to him even though her voice was polite. And there was something else he couldn't get straightened out; the young fellow's attitude had been very strained this morning, he hadn't greeted his daughter with the reception due to her, in fact he had been slightly off-hand. He bent his long length towards Mary Ann and asked her quietly, "Did you mind me keeping the child overnight?"

Mary Ann took a long breath. This man was to be a benefactor, he could make Corny or leave him standing where he was. She should be careful how she answered him about this. But no, she would tell him the truth. "Yes, I did mind, Mr. Blenkinsop. I was nearly demented when Rose Mary was lost and . . . and naturally I wanted her back, but . . . but my husband saw it otherwise. You see, my son hasn't been able to talk, and it's been my husband's theory that he would talk if he was separated from his sister. I've always been against it. Well . . ." She swallowed again. "My husband saw your invitation as a means of keeping them separated for a longer period to . . . to give the boy a chance, as he said. I didn't see it that way. I . . . I was very upset."

Mr. Blenkinsop straightened up and his face was very solemn as he said, "Yes, ma'am. Yes, I can see your point. I can see that you'd be upset. Oh yes." He did not add that he could also see her husband's side of it. It was no use upsetting her still further. "I'm very sorry that I've been the instigator of your worries. I can assure you I wouldn't have enlarged upon them for the world. If only I had known I would have whipped her back here like greased lightning."

Mary Ann's face softened, and she said now, "Thanks. I feel you would have, too."

"I would that. Yes, I would that."

They stood looking at each other for a moment. Then Mr. Blenkinsop said, "Well, I must be on my way, but I'll be seeing you shortly."

"Would you like to stay and have a cup of coffee?"

"No, no thank you, not at the moment. But in the future we'll have odd cups of coffee together no doubt, when the work gets under way." As he turned towards the car he stopped and said, "You're pleased about the factory going up?"

"Yes, oh yes, Mr. Blenkinsop; I'm very pleased."

"Good, good." When he reached the car, he looked over it and said, "Nice little farm you've got here."

"Yes, it's a very nice farm."

"I'd like to come and have a look round some time."

"You'd be very welcome."

"Good-bye, Mrs. Boyle. Please accept my apologies for all this trouble."

"It's quite all right, Mr. Blenkinsop." They nodded to each other, and then she watched him drive away, before slowly walking out of the yard and through the garden to the farmhouse again. As she entered the house Rose Mary's voice came to her, laughter-filled and excited, saying, "Yes, Grandma, I'd have liked to have stayed if David had been there, but I couldn't without David, could I?"

Mary Ann paused in the scullery. She leant against the table and looked down at it. How was she going to explain the situation to Rose Mary? How to tell her that she had to stay here while David remained at home? How? She could put her off for a few hours, but in the end, come this evening, when she knew she wasn't going home she'd have to explain to her in some way. . . . Oh God! Why had this to happen to her, to them all?

11

But before Mary Ann was called upon to explain the situation to Rose Mary she had to explain it to someone else—to Mr. Lord.

It happened round about teatime that Rose Mary came running into the house calling, "Mam! Mam!"

"What is it?" Mary Ann came out of the front room, where she had been sitting alone, leaving Lizzie busy in the kitchen. Lizzie had refused her offer of help, and this, more than anything else since she had come home yesterday, had made her feel, and for the first time in her life, a stranger, a visitor in her home. She had gone into the front room and made a valiant effort not to cry. She met Rose Mary in the hall, and again she said, "What is it?"

Rose Mary was gasping with her running. "It's Mr. Lord, Mam. He says you've got to go up."

"Didn't I tell you not to go anywhere near the house? I told you, didn't I? I told you to keep in the yard."

"But I was in the yard, in the far yard, and Mr. Ben, he waved me up the hill. And when I went up he took me in to Mr. Lord, and Mr. Lord asked if you were still here."

Mary Ann lowered her head, then walked slowly into the kitchen and spoke to her mother.

Lizzie was setting the table. She had her back to Mary Ann, and she kept it like that as Mary Ann said, "He knows I'm here; he wants me to go up."

"You should know by now that you can't keep much from him, and you'd better not try to hide anything from him when you see him."

"It's none of his business."

Now Lizzie did turn round, and her look was hard on her

daughter as she said, "Your life has always been his business, and I'm surprised you have forgotten that."

Again Mary Ann hung her head, and as she did so she became aware of Rose Mary standing to the side of her, her face troubled, her eyes darting between them.

As she turned away, walking slowly towards the door, Rose Mary said, "Can I come with you, Mam?"

"No, stay where you are."

"Are we going home when you come back?"

Mary Ann didn't answer, but as she went out of the back door she heard her mother's voice speaking soothingly to Rose Mary.

Mary Ann entered Mr. Lord's house by the back door, as she always did, and found Ben sitting at the table, preparing his master's tea, buttering thin slices of brown bread, which he would proceed to roll into little pipes. His veined, bony hands had a perpetual shake about them now; he was the same age as his master but he appeared much older; Ben was running down fast. Mary Ann was quick to notice this, and for a moment she forgot her own troubles and the interview that lay before her, and she spoke softly as she said, "Hello, Ben. How are you?"

"Middling, just middling."

"Is Mrs. Rice off to-day?"

"They're always off. Time off, time off, that's all they think of."

"Shall I take the tray in for you?"

"No, no, I can manage." He looked up at her and, his voice dropping, he said, "He's waitin'."

"Very well." She paused a moment longer and added, "You should stop all this; there's no need for it." She waved her hand over the tray. "There's plenty of others to do this; you should have a rest."

"I'll have all the rest I need shortly."

"Oh, Ben, don't say that."

"Go on, go on. I told you, he's waitin'."

As she went through the hall, with its deep-piled red carpet hushing her step, she wondered what he would do without Ben. Ben had been his right arm, also his whipping post, and his outlet; he'd pine without Ben.

She knocked gently on the drawing-room door, and when she was bidden to enter, the scene was as it always remained in her mind. This room never changed; this was Mr. Lord's room. Tony and Lettice had their own sitting-room. It was modernly furnished and very nice, but this room . . . this room had beauty, and dignity, and it was a setting for the figure sitting in the high-backed chair. There was no beauty about Mr. Lord, except that which accompanies age, but there was dignity. It was in his every moment, every look, every glance, whether harsh or soft.

He turned his head towards Mary Ann. Giving her no greeting, he said, without preamble, "You have to be sent for now?"

She did not answer, but walked to the seat opposite to him and, sitting down, said quietly, "How are you?"

"I'm very well. How are you?"

"All right."

"Then if you're all right you should make your face match your mood."

She stared at him; she had never been able to hide anything from him. She turned her gaze to the side now and looked out of the window; then looking back at him, she said, "Have you heard from Tony and Lettice?"

"Yes, I had a letter this morning. They're enjoying their holiday very much."

"And Peter?"

"I understand that he, too, is enjoying himself."

"You will miss him."

"You have to get used to missing people."

"Yes . . . yes, I suppose so." You have to get used to missing people. Would she ever get used to missing Corny? How was it going to end? What was she going to do? . . .

"Well. Now, you've made all the polite enquiries that are necessary to this meeting, you can tell me why you came yesterday and spent the night alone, without either your husband or children?"

She kept her gaze lowered. It was no use saying who told you I came yesterday. Ben was also Mr. Lord's scout; nothing escaped Ben. He might be old and doddery, but his mind was as alert as his master's. From his kitchen window he looked down on to the farm, and on to the road that led to the farm. Few people came or went without Ben's knowledge.

"Have you and Cornelius quarrelled?"

She still kept her head lowered; she still made no sound.

"Look at me!" Mr. Lord's voice was now harsh and commanding. "Tell me what this is all about?"

She did not look at him, but, as she used to do when a child, she pressed her joined hands between her knees and rocked herself slightly as she said, "Rose Mary got lost yesterday. Me grannie came to visit us and upset her. She hid in the boot of a car belonging to an American, a Mr. Blenkinsop. He didn't discover she was there for a long time. We were all searching when Mr. Blenkinsop phoned to say he had found her and he took her to some friends of his. They live in Doncaster. Then, later, he phoned to ask if she could stay the night." She paused here before going on. "I wanted her brought back straightaway, but Corny said it was all right and she could stay."

"Well, well, go on. He said it was all right; he wouldn't have said that if it wasn't all right. Did he know this man?"

"Yes."

"Well then, there would seem little to worry about. But I take it that you didn't like the fact that Rose Mary wasn't coming back right away and so you got into a paddy."

"It isn't as simple as that. You see . . ." She now looked him full in the face. "Corny has always said that David would talk if they were separated. I have always been against it, and when I came home yesterday, I mean after searching for Rose Mary, he was full of the fact that the boy was talking. It must have been the shock of Rose Mary being lost, and Corny said he would have a better chance if they were kept apart a little longer. I thought it was cruel; I still think it is cruel."

Mr. Lord pressed his head back against the chair and screwed his pale-blue eyes up to pin-points. His lips moved from his teeth and he kept his mouth open awhile before he said, "You mean to say that is the reason you left Cornelius?"

"It sounds so simple saying it, but it wasn't like that."

"Stick to the point, child." He still thought of her as a child. "Your husband wants his son to talk; he feels that if he is

120

separated from his sister he will talk. The opportunity presents itself, and no one is going to be any the worse for the experiment, and you mean to say that you took umbrage at this and came home, and stayed the night away from him, purposely. . . . You mean to tell me that this is what it was all about?"

"I tell you it isn't as simple as all that. . . ."

"It is as simple as all that." He leant towards her. Then, moving his index finger slowly at her, he said, "Now, if you know what's good for you, you will get down to the farm quickly, get your things on and make for home."

Mary Ann straightened herself up. "No, no, I can't."

"You mean you're going to remain stubborn."

"I mean I can't; he saw me coming away and he didn't stop me."

"Well, I should say that is something in his favour. I uphold his action. . . . But tell me. How did Rose Mary come here? Did she come by herself?"

"No, he . . . he sent her with . . . with the American. When Mr. Blenkinsop took her home he asked him to bring her here."

Mr. Lord leant back in his chair again, and after a moment he said, "Do you realize, Mary Ann, that this is serious? Situations like this lead to explosions. Now, you do as I tell you." He did not say take my advice; this was an order. "Get yourself away home this very minute, and try to remember that you're not dealing with a silly boy, but a strong-willed man. I've reason to know the strength of Mr. Cornelius Boyle. Twice in my life I've come up against it. Because he cares for you deeply you might bend his will, but don't try to bend it too far. For, if you do, you'll break yourself and your little family. . . . Come here." He held out his hand and she rose slowly and went to him, and when she stood by his side he took hold of her arm, and, looking up at her, he said, "Don't destroy something good. And you have something good in your marriage. As you know, he wasn't the one I wanted for you, but one learns that one is sometimes wrong. Cornelius is the man for you. Now promise me," he said, "you'll go home."

Mary Ann moved her head from side to side. She pulled in her bottom lip, then muttered under her breath, "I can't, I can't."

With a surprisingly strong and swift movement she was thrust aside, and, his voice angry now, he cried at her, "You're a little fool! Now, I'm warning you. Start learning now before it's too late. If you make him swallow his pride you'll regret it to your dying day, but you'll gain if you swallow yours. Have sense. . . . Go on, get away, get out of my sight."

She got out of his sight. Slowly she closed the door after her and walked through the hall and to the kitchen. There Ben raised his eyes but not his head, and neither of them spoke.

She did not immediately return to the farmhouse but went up a by-lane and stood leaning against the five-barred gate that led into the long field. Her whole being ached. She wanted to cry and cry and cry; she felt lonely, lost and frightened. But she couldn't go back. He had let her come away when he could easily have stopped her if he had wanted to. If he had cared enough he could have stopped her. She had been in paddies before and he had talked her out of them, coaxed her out of them. He had always brought her round, sometimes none too gently. Once he had slapped her behind, as he would a child, because he said she was acting like one. That had made her more wild still. They hadn't spoken for a whole day then, but come night time and in bed his hand had sought hers and she had left it there within his big palm.

But she couldn't go back, she couldn't, because what he had done to her was cruel. She had nearly been demented when Rose Mary was missing, and no matter how much stock he had put on his theory of David talking if they were separated, he should have forgone that, knowing the state she was in, knowing how she longed to see Rose Mary again and to feel that she was really safe. But all he could think about was that he had been right, and David was talking. She was glad, oh yes, she was glad that David was talking; and now once he had started he would go on. There had been no need to keep them apart; no matter what he said there had been no need to do what he had done. He had been cruel, cruel, and she couldn't go back, not . . . not unless he came for her.

12

But Corny did not come for her, and now it was Tuesday and the situation had become terrifying. Her da had been over to the house; Michael had been over to the house; and when they had come back neither of them had said a word, and she had been too proud to ask what had transpired.

Then to-day her mother had been over. She hadn't known she was going; it was the last thing on earth she thought her mother would do, to go and talk to Corny. Now Lizzie was sitting with a cup of tea in her hand and she looked down at it as she said, "You'll have to make the first move."

"What if I don't?"

"Well, that's up to you; it's your life."

"Why should I be the one to make the first move?"

"Because you're in the wrong."

"Oh, Ma!" Mary Ann was on her feet. "You're another one. Everybody's taken his part, everybody. It's fantastic. Nobody sees my side of it and what I went through, what agony I went through when Rose Mary was lost."

"We know all about that." Lizzie took a sip from her cup. "But that's beside the point now; the whole issue, to my mind, is the fact that you've always been against the twins being separated even for a few hours. Now, if you'd only been sensible about that, this whole business would never have happened. And another thing, Corny was absolutely right, the child's really talking. Four days they've been separated and he's chattering away like a magpie." Lizzie now leaned towards Mary Ann and repeated, "Chattering. It's like a small miracle to hear him. And that alone should make you realize that you've been in the wrong, girl."

"All right, all right." Mary Ann flung her arm wide. "He's

proved his point, he's right. But that's just the outside of things; there was the way this was done, and the time it was done, and how I felt. Isn't that to be taken into consideration?"

"You're not the only one who's felt like this; I nearly went mad when you were lost, remember. All mothers feel like this."

"Aw, you're just twisting it, you won't go deeper. And another thing." Mary Ann bounced her head towards Lizzie now. "You don't want me here. Oh I know, I can tell, but don't worry, you won't have to put up with me much longer, I can get a job anytime."

Lizzie, ignoring the first part of Mary Ann's small tirade, said quietly, "And you'll let Rose Mary go back home?"

"No, I won't."

"Who's keeping them separated now? And that child's fretting. She's hardly eaten a peck in two days; she's got to go back to that boy, not because of him but for her own sake. David's not worrying so much. He asked for her, but that's all. He's as bright as a cricket. Do you know where he was when I got there? Under a car with Corny, and thick with oil, and as happy as a sandboy."

Mary Ann walked towards the window. She wanted to say sarcastically: was Corny as happy as a sandboy too? But she couldn't mention his name. Her mother hadn't said anything about Corny. She was acting like her da, and their Michael, in this. They were all for him. Yes, even her da now. It was fantastic; everybody was for Corny and against her. She swung round from the window, saying, "Well, I'm not crawling back, Ma, no matter what you say or any of you. As I said, I'll get a job."

As she stumped past her mother on her way across the room to the hall, Lizzie said quietly, "Don't be such a fool, girl. The trouble with you is that you have done the manoeuvring and fixing all your life, so much so, until you've come to think that things have to be done your way or not at all."

"Oh, Ma!" Mary Ann turned an accusing face on Lizzie.

"You can say Oh, Ma! like that, but it's true. Now you've come up against something you can't have fixed on your terms. Corny's a man; he's not your da, or Mr. Lord, or Tony, he's your husband; and he has his rights, and I'm warning you. You try to make him crawl and you'll regret it all your days."

Mary Ann banged the door after her. Her ma had said practically the same words as Mr. Lord. What was the matter with everybody? They were treating her like someone who had committed a crime. She had rights too. Or hadn't she any right to rights? The equality of the sexes. That made you laugh. . . . Bunkum! It was all right on paper, but when it was put into action, look what happened. Everybody took the man's side, even her mother. . . . She couldn't get over that. She could understand her da in a way, him being a man, but her mother! She was for him, up to the neck and beyond. Everybody was for him and against her.

Then the next morning Fanny came.

Mike ushered her in, unexpectedly, through the back door, crying, "Liz! Liz! Look at this stupid, fat old bitch walking all the way up from the bus. Hadn't the sense to let us know she was coming, and we could have picked her up. . . . Get in there with you."

Mary Ann was entering the kitchen from the hall, and she saw her mother rush down the long room and greet Fanny at the scullery door, saying, "Oh, hello there, Fan. Why didn't you tell us?"

"Now, why should I, Lizzie? I've a pair of pins on me yet; and when the doctor said it would do me good to lose some of me fat, do a bit more walking, I said to him, 'Now where the hell do you think I'm going to walk . . . round and round the block?' 'No,' he said; 'get yourself out for a day or so. Take a dander into the country, a bus ride, and then a wee stroll.' I thought to meself at the time that's Mike and Liz getting at him . . . did you get at him?"

Lizzie and Mike were laughing loudly, and they both shook their heads, and Mike said, "No, we didn't get at him. But we wish we had thought of it, if it would have brought you out more often. There, sit yourself down."

He helped her to lower her great fat body into a chair while saying to Rose Mary, "Let her be now. Let her get her puff."

Rose Mary, moving aside, looked towards her mother and cried, "Me Great-gran!"

Fanny turned her eyes and looked across the room now towards Mary Ann and said, "That's just in case you can't see me, Mary Ann, just in case."

Mary Ann smiled and came forward and, standing by her friend's side, she said simply, "Hello."

"Hello, hinny." Fanny patted her hand; then asked, "How are you keepin'?"

"All right."

"Good, good." Fanny nodded her head.

Her questions and attitude as yet gave Mary Ann no indication that she knew anything about . . . the trouble, yet it took an event of importance to get Fanny away from the fortress of her home in Mulhattan's Hall, that almost derelict, smelly dark house, divided into flats, one consisting of two rooms in which Fanny had lived since she was married, in which she had brought into the world twelve children, all of whom had gone from her now, some not to return, although they were still living. Jarrow Council had not got down yet to demolishing Burton Street and Mulhattan's Hall, but they would surely come to it before they finished the new Jarrow, and Mary Ann often hoped that Fanny would die before that day, for surely if she didn't she would go when Mulhattan's Hall went.

"Here," said Lizzie; "drink that up."

"And what's this?"

"Don't ask the road you know, get it down you," said Lizzie, speaking brusquely to this old friend of hers; and Fanny, sniffing at the glass, smiled and, looking sideways at Lizzie, said, "Brandy, I'm glad I came." Then, putting the glass to her lips, she threw off the drink at one go, gave a slight shudder, then placed the glass back in Lizzie's hand, saying, "Thanks, Lass."

"Look," put in Mike. "Now that you've got this far and we're in this lovely weather why don't you stay for a day or two?"

"Mike, I'm getting the four o'clock bus back. I've said it and that's what I'm going to do. But thanks all the same for the invitation."

126

"You're a cantankerous old bitch still." He pushed her head none too gently with the flat of his hand, and she retaliated by bringing her hand across his thigh with a resounding wallop. "There," she said. "An' there's more where that comes from. Now get yourself away about your business with your female family, go on."

All except Mary Ann were laughing now, and as Mike made for the door he replied, "Me family's not all females; there's a definite male element in it, and I'm expecting two results of his efforts at any minute now."

"Aw, the poor animals, they don't get away with much, like ourselves. What do you say, Lizzie?"

Lizzie smiled gently as she said, "I'd say, give me your hat and coat now that you've got your breath and get yourself settled in the big chair there." She pointed to Mike's leather chair at the side of the fireplace. "Then you'll have a cup of tea and a bite that'll put you over till dinner time."

If Mary Ann at first had wondered what had brought her friend to the farm, half-an-hour later she was in no doubt whatever, because, of all the topics touched upon, Corny's name or that of David had not been mentioned, and when her mother, holding her hand out towards Rose Mary, said, "I'm going to the dairy, I want some cream. Come along with me," Mary Ann knew that Mrs. McBride was being given the opportunity to voice the real reason for her visit.

Mary Ann was standing at the long kitchen table in the centre of the room preparing a salad, and Fanny was looking at her from out of the depths of the leather chair, and for a full minute after being left alone neither of them spoke, until Fanny said abruptly, "I don't blame you, lass. Don't think that."

Mary Ann turned her head swiftly over her shoulder and looked at this fat, kindly, wise, bigoted, obstinate, and sometimes harsh old woman, and after a pause she asked, "How did you find out?"

"Oh, bad news has the speed of light. I read that somewhere, and it's true. It was last night, comin' out of confession, I met Jimmy's mother. She's got a mouth on her like a whale. She didn't know the real rights of the case, she said, but she said you were gone to your mother's because she was ill, and you had taken the girl with you, leavin' the boy behind you. She thought it was a funny thing to do as Jimmy had said you couldn't separate the two with a pair of pliers. What did I think of it, she said. Was it all right between them; they weren't splitting up or anything? I said to her, when I heard that the Holy family was splitting up then I'd know for sure that my grandson and his wife were following suit. . . . But I was worried sick, lass, sick to the soul of me. I knew that something must have happened for you to separate the children, an' so I went along this mornin'."

Mary Ann was standing with her buttocks pressed against the back of the table. She moved her head in small jerks before she said, "You've been home already to-day?"

"Aye, I got there around half-past nine, and, when I got to the bottom of things, let him take what I gave him."

Mary Ann stared at Mrs. McBride, her lower lip hanging loose. Corny was the pride and joy of this old woman's heart. In Mrs. McBride's eyes Corny was all that a man should be, physically, mentally and morally. Her standards might not be those of Olympus but they were high, and she knew what went to make a good man, and she had always considered that her grandson, Corny, had all the ingredients for the pattern in her mind. Yet here she was, against Corny, and the first one to be so.

Everybody had been against her. They had said: You're a fool. It's your temper. It's your stubbornness. You can't have everything your own way, and you've got to realize that. But nobody, up till now, had said that Corny was at fault. Yet here was his grannie shouting him down.

"I told him he was a big, empty-headed nowt, and he didn't know which side his bread was buttered, and that if you never went back to him he was only gettin' what he deserved."

"Oh, Mrs. McBride!" It was a mere whisper, and Mary Ann's head drooped as she spoke.

"Well!" Fanny was sitting upright now, as upright as her fat would allow. "When he told me what it was all about I nearly went straight through the roof. A man! I said. You call yourself a man, and you take the pip at a thing like that. Just because she expresses her opinion you go off the deep end?"

Mary Ann raised her head slightly. "I . . . I said things I shouldn't have, Mrs. McBride; he's . . . he's not altogether to blame. I . . . I said I hated him."

"Aw!" Mrs. McBride pushed her fat round in the chair until she was half-turned away from Mary Ann, and, looking into the empty fireplace, she thrust her arm out and flapped her hand towards Mary Ann as she cried, "Aw, if a man is going to let his wife walk out on him because she says she hates him, then every other house in the land would be empty. I've never heard anything so childish in me life. Hate him! I'd like a penny for every time I've said I hated McBride. And mind . . ." She twisted herself round again in Mary Ann's direction, and, her arm again extended and her fingers wagging, she said, "I always accompanied me words with something concrete, the frying pan, the flat iron, a bottle, anything that came to hand. You know me big black broth pan, the one I can hardly lift off the hob when it's full? I can just about manage it when it's empty. Well, I remember the day as if it was yesterday that I hurled it at his head, and I used those very words to give it God speed: I hate you. And I didn't say them plain and unadorned, if you get what I mean; I always made me remarks to McBride a bit flowery. Be god!" She moved her triple chins from one shoulder to the other. "If that pan had found its target that particular day it would have been good-bye to McBride twenty years earlier. Aw! Me aim was poor that time. An' it was likely because I was carryin'. I gave birth to me twins three days later. One of them died, the other one is Georgie, you know."

Mary Ann wanted to smile; she wanted to laugh; she wanted to cry; oh, how she wanted to cry.

"Come here," said Fanny gently. "Come here." And Mary Ann went to her, and Fanny put her arms round her waist and said, "I'm upset to me very soul. He's as near to me as the blood pumping out of me heart, but at the same time I'm not for him. No, begod! The way I see it is, he was given a pot of gold and he's acted as if it was a holey bucket picked up off a midden. He let you walk away . . . just like that." She made a slow gliding movement with her hand.

"B . . . b . . . but, Mrs. McBride. . . ."

"Oh, I don't blame you for walkin' out, I don't blame you, not a jot, lass. You've got to make a stand with them or your life's simply hell. Even when you do make a stand it isn't easy, but if you let them walk over you you might as well go straight to the priest and arrange for a requiem to be said, because your time's short. You can bank on that."

Mary Ann stood quietly now, fondling the creased and not over-clean hand as she asked, "How was he? And David?"

"Oh, a bit peakish-looking about the gills. They all get very sorry for themselves. He'd been having his work cut out getting the breakfast ready; the place was strewn with dishes. Hell's cure to you, I said. You're just gettin' what you deserve. But David, he was sprightly. He speaks now. I got the gliff of me life."

Mary Ann's hand stopped moving over Mrs. McBride. "It was about that that all the trouble started."

"About David talkin', you mean?"

"Yes, Corny had said that if they were separated David would talk. . . . Well he's been proved right, hasn't he?"

"Nonsense, nonsense. It was the scare he got when Rose Mary was lost that made him talk, not the separation."

"Yes, I know. But Corny thought that if they came together too quickly that David wouldn't make any more effort. And I can see his point, I can, Mrs. McBride, but——"

"Now don't you go soft, girl. No matter what points you see, don't you go soft, because you'll have to pay for it in the end. He's a big, ignorant, empty-headed nowt, as I told him, an' I should know because he's inherited a lot of meself." She nodded at Mary Ann, and Mary Ann was forced to smile just the slightest.

It was funny about people. They never acted as you expected them to. She had really been afraid of Mrs. McBride finding out and going for her, and yet here she was taking her part. She bent down swiftly and kissed the flabby, wrinkled face, and Fanny held her and said, "There now. There now. Now don't cry, he's not worth it. Although it's meself that's sayin' it, he's not worth it."

At the same time, deep in her heart, Fanny was praying, "God forgive me. God forgive me for every word I've uttered against him in these last few minutes."

It was the evening of the same day, when Mary Ann was in the bathroom bathing Rose Mary, when she heard the car stop in the lane outside the front door. Rose Mary, too, heard it, and she looked up at her mother and said, "There's a car, Mam."

Mary Ann's heart began to pound and she had trouble in controlling her voice as she said, "Come on, get out and get dried."

"Mam." Rose Mary hugged the towel around her. "Do you think it'll be me . . . ?"

"Get dried and put your nightie on. Come on. Here, sit on the cracket and give me your feet." She rubbed Rose Mary's feet vigorously; she rubbed her back, and her chest. She had put her nightdress on and combed her hair when the bathroom door was pushed open and Lizzie stood there, saying, "You'd better come down; there's an assortment down there wanting to see you."

Mary Ann's eyes widened. "An assortment? Who? What?"

"Well, come and see for yourself. Five of them, headed by that Jimmy from the garage."

A cold wave of disappointment swept through her, making her shiver.

"What do they want?" she said.

"You, apparently."

"Me! What do they want with me?"

"You'd better come down and see."

"Can I come, Mam?"

"No, stay where you are. Go and get into bed."

"But, Mam."

"Get into bed, Rose Mary."

She turned from her daughter and passed her mother; then ran down the stairs and to the front door. And it was as Lizzie had said, it was an assortment that stood on the front lawn facing her.

She knew for certain that Jimmy was a boy, but she had first of all to guess at the sex of the other four. True they were wearing trousers, but there ended any indication of their maleness, for they were also wearing an assortment of blouses, one with a ruffle at the neck; their hair was long and ranged from starling blond to tow colour, from dead brown to a horrible ginger. There wasn't a hair to be seen on their faces, nor yet on what skin was showing of their arms. The sight of them repulsed Mary Ann and made her stomach heave. She turned her attention pointedly to Jimmy, and noticed in this moment that although his hair, too, was longish, his maleness stood out from that of his pals like a sore finger.

Jimmy grinned at her. "Hello, Mrs. Boyle," he said.

"What do you want, Jimmy?" Mary Ann's tone was curt.

"Aw, I just thought I'd pop along and see you. You know, about . . . about the lines you did. You know."

"Oh!" Mary Ann closed her eyes for a moment and wet her lips. She had forgotten about the lines. She wanted to say, "Look, I'm not interested any more," but Jimmy's bright expression prevented her from flattening him with such a remark.

"These are me pals . . . the Group. This is Duke." He thumbed towards the repulsive, red-haired individual. "He runs us and he's good at tunes. I was tellin' you." He nodded twice, then thumbed towards the next boy. "This is Barney. He's on the drums." Barney was the tow-haired one. He was also the one with the ruffle. He opened his mouth wide and smiled at Mary Ann. She had never seen such a big mouth on a boy before. It seemed to split his face in two. She turned her eyes to the next boy as Jimmy said, "This is Poodle Patter. We call him that 'cos he's good at ad lib, small talk you know, keeping things goin'. Aren't you, Poodle?"

Poodle jerked his head at Mary Ann, and a ripple passed over his face. It was an expression of self-satisfaction and had no connection whatever with a pleased-to-meet-you expression.

Mary Ann stared at Poodle, at his startlingly blond hair, and she had to stop her nose from wrinkling in this case.

"And he's Dave." Jimmy thumbed towards the back of the group, where stood the brown-haired individual. He had small merry eyes and a thin mouth, and he nodded to Mary Ann and said, "Wat-cher!"

"Dave plays the guitar, and he can do the mouth-organ."

Jimmy jerked his head towards Dave, and Dave jerked his head back at him, and they exchanged grins.

Mary Ann was tired; she was weary with worry; she was sick at this moment with disappointment; she had thought, oh, she had thought that Corny had come for her; and now she was sick in another way as she looked at these four boys. Jimmy didn't make her sick, he only irritated her. She said to him, "Look, Jimmy, I'm very busy. What do you want?"

Jimmy's long face lengthened; his eyebrows went up and his lower lip went down, and he said, "Well, like I said, about your lyrics. Duke's put a tune to them."

"Oh!"

"Haven't you, Duke?"

Duke now stepped forward. He had an insolent walk; he had an insolent look; and he spread his look all over Mary Ann before he said, "It was ropey in parts."

"What was?"

"Well, that stuff that you did. The title's all right, and the punch line, 'She acts like a woman,' but the bit about not wantin' diamonds and mink, well, that isn't with it, not the day. They don't expect them things. A drink, aye, but not the other jollop."

"No?" The syllable sounded aggressive, even to Mary Ann herself.

"No! Not the teenagers don't. Who's going to buy them furs an' rings and things, eh? Unless a fellow hits the jackpot he can just scramble by by hisself." Duke now wrinkled his nose as if from a bad smell. "Aw, it's old fashioned. Ten years, even twenty behind the times. But I've left in about the rings. But they don't talk like you wrote it any more; still the way I've worked it, it'll come over."

"Thank you."

"The pleasure's mine."

Mary Ann's jaws tightened. They don't talk like you wrote it any more. How old did he think she was, forty?

"Well, how do they talk?" The aggressive note was still there.

"Huh!" Duke laughed, then slanted his eyes around his mates, and they all joined in, with the exception of Jimmy, for Jimmy was looking at the bad weather signs coming from Mrs. Boyle. He knew Mrs. Boyle's bad weather signs.

"Want me to tell you?"

Before Mary Ann could answer Jimmy put in, "Aw, give over, Duke. You know you like it; you said it had it, especially that line."

"Oh aye, I've just said, that's a punch line: 'She acts like a woman.' But the rest . . . aw, it's old men's stuff . . . Bob Hope, Bing Crosby."

"Well, there's nothing more to be said, is there?" Mary Ann had a great desire to reach out and slap his face. She turned quickly away. But as she did so Jimmy put his hand out towards her, saying, "Aw, Mrs. Boyle, that's just him. Don't take any notice; he's always like this. But he likes it, he does." He turned his head over his shoulder and said to Duke, "Come off it, Duke, an' tell her you think it's good. We all think it's good." He swung his gaze over the rest of them, and the other three boys nodded and spoke together, and the gist was that they thought the lyrics fine and with it, just a word had needed altering here and there.

"You see." Jimmy nodded at Mary Ann. "Would you like to hear it?"

"No, Jimmy." Mary Ann's tone was modified now, and she added swiftly, "I'm . . . I'm busy."

"Aw, come on, Mrs. Boyle; that's what we've come out for, to let you hear it. And then if you think it's all right we was goin' to try it out at 'The Well' on Saturday night. An' you never know, there's always scouts hanging round an' they might pick it up."

Mary Ann looked from Jimmy to Duke, and back to Jimmy, and she said, stiffly now, "That wasn't my idea; I thought it could be sent away to——"

"You do what you like, missus," Duke put in, shaking his head vigorously, "but if you send it away that's the last you'll hear of it, until you recognize snatches of the tune on the telly and hear your words all mixed up. You send it away if you like, but it's as Jimmy says, there are scouts kickin' around, on the look-out for punch lines, an' you've got one here, 'She acts like a woman'. It's got a two-fold attraction; it'll appeal to the old dames over twenty, and make the young 'uns think they're grown up. See what I mean?" Duke was speaking ordinarily now, and Mary Ann nodded and said, flatly, "Yes, I suppose you're right." But she wished they would get themselves away. She was still feeling sick with disappointment. She wanted to be alone and cry. Oh, how she wanted to cry at this minute. What was she standing here for anyway? As long as she remained they wouldn't budge. She was turning round when Jimmy pleaded, "Will you listen to it, then?" His face was one big appeal, and before Mary Ann could answer, and without taking his eyes off her, he said, "Get the kit out."

The four boys stared at Mary Ann for a minute, then turned nonchalantly about and went towards the car, and Mary Ann, looking helplessly at Jimmy, said, "Where are they going to do it?"

"Why, here." Jimmy spread his hands. "We can play anywhere."

Mary Ann cast a glance over her shoulder. There was only her mother in the house; her da and their Michael were still on the farm; they were having a bit of trouble getting a cow to calve. If they had been indoors she would have said a firm no to any demonstration, but now she just stood and looked at Jimmy, then from him to where the boys were hauling their instruments out of the car.

Jimmy brought his attention back to her when he said, softly, "I miss you back at the house, Mrs. Boyle."

She looked at his straight face and it was all she could do not to burst into tears right there.

"It isn't the same."

"Be quiet, Jimmy."

It was no use trying to hoodwink Jimmy by telling him she was staying with her mother because she was sick, or some such tale, for behind Jimmy's comic expression Mary Ann now felt, as Corny had always pointed out, there was a serious side, a knowing side. Jimmy wasn't as soppy as he made himself out to be. Even a few minutes ago, when he had pointed to Duke as the leader of the group, she felt that whatever brains were needed to guide this odd assortment it was he who supplied them.

The boys came back up the path, and one of them handed a

guitar to Jimmy; then, grouping themselves, they faced her and, seemingly picking up an invisible sign, they all started together. There followed a blast of sound, a combination of instruments and voices that was deafening.

SHE ACTS LIKE A WOMAN
SHE ACTS LIKE A WOMAN

Mary Ann screwed up her face against the noise. She watched the fair-haired boy, Poodle Patter as Jimmy had called him, his head back, wobbling on the last word: WOOMA . . . AN. This was followed by a number of chords, and then they all started again.

MAN, I'M TELLING YOU.
SHE ACTS LIKE A WOMAN.

SHE PELTED ME WITH THINGS,
AND THEN SHE TORE HER HAIR.

SHE ACTS LIKE A WOMAN.

I'VE GIVEN HER MY LOT,
NOW I WAS FINISHED, BROKE,
AND THEN SHE SPOKE OF LOVE.

SHE ACTS LIKE A WOMAN.

ME, SHE SAID, SHE WANTED,
NOT RINGS OR THINGS.

SHE ACTS LIKE A WOMAN.

MAN, I JUST SPREAD MY HANDS.
WHAT WAS I TO DO?
YOU TELL ME,
WHAT WAS I TO DO?
EARLY MORNING THERE SHE STOOD,
NO MAKE-UP FACE LIKE MUD,
BIG EYES RAINING TEARS AND FEARS.

SHE ACTS LIKE A WOMAN.

THEN, MAN, SOMETHING MOVED IN HERE,
LIKE DAYLIGHT,
AND I COULD SEE SHE ONLY WANTED M-EE.

SHE ACTS LIKE A WOOO-MA-AN.

As the voices trailed off the last word and all the hands crashed out the last note, Mary Ann gaped at the five boys, and they stood in silence waiting. For a brief second she forgot her misery. It had sounded grand, excellent, as good as anything that was on the pops. He was clever. She looked directly at Duke and said what she thought.

"I think you've made a splendid job of it, the way you've arranged the words and brought out that line. I think it's grand."

All the faces before her were expanding now into wide, pleased grins. Even Duke's cockiness was lost under the outward sign of his pleasure, when, at that moment, round the corner of the house, came Mike. He came like a bolt of thunder.

"What the hell do you think you're up to! What's this?"

After the words had crashed about them they all turned and looked at the big fellow who was coming towards them, his step slower now, his face showing an expression of sheer incredulity. They stood silent as he eyed them from head to toe, one after the other. Then, his voice exploding again, he cried, "What the hell are you lot doing here? Who's dug you up?"

"Da . . . Da, this is Jimmy. You know Jimmy."

Mike turned his eyes towards Jimmy; then returned them slowly back to the other four as Mary Ann went on hastily, "They are Jimmy's Group; they've . . ." She paused. How to say they had set some of her words to music; this wasn't the time. "They had a tune they thought I . . . I would like to hear."

"THEY . . . HAD . . . A . . . TUNE they thought you'd like to hear? Have you gone barmy, girl? You call that noise a tune? It's nearly put the finishing touches to Freda."

"Then Freda isn't with it, is she, Mister?" This was Duke speaking. His tone was insolent and brought Mike swinging round to him. "Freda's more with it than you, young fellow, if that is what you are, which I doubt very much. Freda's only a cow, a sick cow at the present moment, but I wouldn't swap her for the lot of you."

The four boys stared back at Mike, their faces expressionless. It was a tense moment, until the fair-haired boy, Poodle Patter, asked quietly, "What she sick with, Mister?"

"She's trying to calve, but you lot wouldn't understand anything about that, being neither one thing nor the other."

Again there was a silence, during which Mary Ann's hand went out towards Mike. But she didn't touch him; she was afraid she might explode something here, for she could see him tearing his one arm from her grasp and knocking them down like ninepins.

"You'd be surprised." This calm rejoinder came from Duke. "As me dad says, ministers wear frocks but they still manage to be fathers."

Mike and Duke surveyed each other for a moment. Then Mike, his lips hardly moving, said, "Get yourselves out! An' quick."

For answer, Duke lifted one shoulder and turned about, and the others followed suit, Jimmy coming up in the rear. As they neared the gate Poodle stopped, swung round, and, his face wearing a most innocent expression, addressed Mike, calling up the path to him, "Can you tell me, Mister, if the caps are put on the milk bottles after the cows lay them, or do they all come through sealed up?"

Mary Ann's two hands now flashed out and caught Mike's sleeve, and she begged softly under her breath, "Da! Da! Don't, please."

Outside the gate and standing near the car, Duke turned again and looked up towards Mike, and he called in a loud voice now, "If you'd started anything, old 'un, you'd have come off second best, an' if you hadn't been a cripple with only one hand I wouldn't have let you get away with half what you did. But don't try it on again."

Mary Ann leant back and hung on to Mike now, and as she did so Lizzie and Michael appeared at the other side of him, and Lizzie said, tersely, "Let them go. Let them go. Come on, get yourself inside." They pulled him around and almost dragged him indoors.

138

Neither of them had said a word to Mary Ann, and she stood leaning against the stanchion of the door, looking at the car, waiting for it to go, and as she watched she saw Jimmy spring out and come up to the path again. And this brought her agitatedly from the doorway and hastily towards him, crying under her breath, "Get yourself away; get them out of this."

"All right, all right, Mrs. Boyle; they'll do nothin'. I'm sorry. I'm sorry about all this, but you see I didn't only come about the tune, there . . . there was something else. It was . . . well, I won't be seeing you again, I don't suppose. That's what I meant to say first of all."

Mary Ann shook her head, and the boy went on, "You see, I'm leavin'."

Mary Ann forced herself to say, "I'm sorry," and was about to add yet again, "Get yourself and that crowd away," when Jimmy put in, "So am I, but with the boss s . . . sellin' up. . . ."

"What! What did you say?" She put her hand out towards him as if she was going to grab the lapel of his coat. Then she closed her fist and pressed it into her other hand and almost whimpered, "Selling up. What do you mean?"

"Well, that's what I came about. You see, I think the boss is goner sell out to Mr. Blenkinsop. He wouldn't sell out to Riley, 'cos he doesn't like Mr. Riley, does he? But . . . but I think he'll sell out to the American. And I wouldn't want to stay if the boss wasn't there, so I'm lookin' out for another job. . . ."

"Who . . . who told you this?"

"Oh. Well, you know me; I keep me ears open, Mrs. Boyle." He stared at her, his long face unsmiling. "It's awful back there without you. An' I don't think the boss can stick it, that's why he's goin' I suppose."

There was a loud concerted call from the car now, and Jimmy said, "I'll have to be off, but . . . but that's really what I came about. Bye, Mrs. Boyle."

She nodded at him and then said under her breath, "Goodbye, Jimmy."

She watched the car move away in a cloud of black smoke from the exhaust, and when it was out of sight she still stood where Jimmy had left her. It was many, many years since she had experienced the feeling of utter despair, and then it had been her da who had evoked that feeling in her. Yet she could recall that her despair in the past had always been threaded with hope, hope that something nice would happen to her da. And nice things had happened to her da. Bad things had also happened to him, but in the main they were nice things that had happened. He stood where he was to-day because of the nice things she had wished and prayed would happen to him. She had always worked at her wishing and her praying—she had never let God get on with it alone—and so her da had made good.

But now she had reached a point in her existence where the main issue was not somebody else's life but her own; she could see her life disintegrating, crumbling away before her eyes. How had it started? How had this situation come about? How did all such situations come about but by little things piling on little things. One stick, one straw, one piece of wood, all entwined; another stick, another straw, another piece of wood, and soon you had a little dam; and a little dam grew with every layer until it stretched across the river of your life and you were cut off, cut off from the other part of you, that part of you that held your heart, and, in her case, cut off from her own flesh and blood, from her son. But the son, in this moment, was a secondary loss; it was the father she was thinking about; Corny was going to sell up. He had stood fast from the beginning; he had bought the garage in the face of opposition. Everybody had said he had been done. Four thousand for a place like that! He must have been bonkers, was the general opinion. Oh yes, it would be a good thing if the road went through, but would it go through? Corny had held on, held on to the thread-bare hope of the road going through. And the road hadn't gone through, yet still he had held on. Something would turn up, something; he knew it would. She could feel him stroking her hair in the darkness of the night, talking faith into himself, re-charging himself for another day. "You'll see, Mary Ann, you'll see. Something 'll turn up, and then I'll make it all up to you. I'll buy you the biggest car you ever saw. I'll have the house rebuilt; you'll have so many new clothes that Lettice will think she's a rag-woman." Corny, in the dark of the night, talking faith into himself and her. And now he was going to sell up. He couldn't, he couldn't.

"What's come over you?"

Mary Ann turned and looked up the path to where Michael was standing in the doorway, so like his father that he could be his younger brother. She did not answer him but walked towards him, her face grim with the defiance his tone had evoked in her.

"How in the name of God have you got yourself mixed up with that lot?"

"I'm not mixed up with that lot; I've never seen them in my life before, except Jimmy."

She glared at him as she passed him, and she was going across the hall when his voice came to her, softly now, saying, "You take my advice and get yourself off home this very minute. Don't be such a blasted little fool."

"You mind your own business, our Michael. You're so blooming smug you make me sick."

"And you're so blooming pig-headed you're messing up your life. Corny is right in the stand he's taking. Everybody is with him."

She was at the foot of the stairs now, and she turned to face him, crying, "I don't care if the whole world is with him. I don't need your sympathy or anybody else's. I can stand on my own feet. And you mind your own business and gather all your forces to run your own life. You're not dead yet; you may have a long way to go, so don't crow."

She was at the top of the stairs when Michael's voice came from the foot, crying at her, "Who's crowing? Be your age, and stop acting like little Mary Ann Shaughnessy."

As Mary Ann burst into her room she heard her mother's voice crying, "Michael!" and his voice trailing away, saying, "Aw well, somebody's got to. . . ."

And then she was brought to a stop by the sight of Rose Mary standing near the window. She was looking straight at her, her face tear-stained and her lips trembling. "I saw Jimmy, Mam," she said.

"Get into bed. I told you to get into bed."

"I want to go back home, Mam."

"Get into bed, Rose Mary."

"I want our David, Mam, and me dad. I miss them. I miss our David, Mam."

"Rose Mary, what did I say?"

"Could I just go over the morrow and——?"

Mary Ann's hand came none too gently across Rose Mary's buttocks, and Rose Mary let out a loud cry, and when the hand came again she let out another. A minute later the door burst open and there stood Lizzie.

"You've got no need to take it out of the child. Michael was right; you've got to come to your senses. And don't you smack her again; she's done nothing. The only thing she wants is to go home to her father and her brother."

"She happens to be my child, Mother." Mary Ann always addressed Lizzie as mother in times of stress. "And I'll do what I like with her, as you did with me."

"Well, you smack her again if you dare!" Lizzie's face was dark with temper, and Mary Ann's equally so as she snapped back, "I'll smack her when I like. She happens to be mine, and I'll thank you not to interfere. And I'd better inform you now that this is the last night you'll have to give me shelter; I'm going to find a place for us both to-morrow."

"You're mad, girl, that's what you are, mad. It's a pity Corny didn't use his hands on you and beat sense into you. He's slipped up somewhere."

The door banged and Mary Ann turned slowly round to see her daughter sitting up in bed, her face puckered, her arms held out towards her, and, rushing to her, she hugged her to her breast. Then throwing herself on the bed, she cradled the child in her arms and they both cried together.

13

The following morning Mary Ann went to Newcastle, and she took Rose Mary with her. Lizzie had shed tears in front of her before she left the house, saying, "Don't be silly, lass, don't be silly. We've all said things we're sorry for, but it's just because we're all concerned for you."

She had replied to her mother, "It's all right, it's all right, I know." She had sounded very subdued, and she was very subdued. Inside, she felt lifeless, half dead. She left Lizzie with the impression that she was going after a job, and she was, but it wasn't the real reason for her visit to Newcastle.

First, she must go and see Mr. Quinton. It was many years since she had seen Bob Quinton. At different periods in her life he had loomed large, and when he appeared on her horizon it had always spelt trouble, mostly for her da, because her da had thought Mr. Quinton wanted her ma, and he had at one time. But all that was in the past. She was going to Mr. Quinton now to ask him how she could get in touch with Mr. Blenkinsop.

Mary Ann was not shown into Mr. Quinton's presence immediately. The girl in the enquiries office wanted to know her business, and when she said it was private, the girl stared at her, then she took her time before she lifted the receiver and began to speak.

Mary Ann's spirits were so low at this moment that she couldn't take offence.

When the girl stopped speaking she looked up at Mary Ann and said, "Miss Taylor will see if he's in; you had better take a seat."

Mary Ann had hardly sat herself down and pulled Rose Mary's coat straight when the phone rang again, and the girl, looking up, said, "He'll see you."

It was almost at the same moment that Mary Ann heard a remembered voice coming from the adjoining room. The intersecting door was opened by a woman, and, behind her, appeared Mr. Quinton. "Well, hello, Mary Ann." He held out his hand as he crossed towards her.

"Hello, Mr. Quinton."

"Oh, it is good to see you. It's years since I clapped eyes on you." He held on to her hand. "And this, I bet, is Rose Mary. When was it I last saw her?" He bent down to Rose Mary. "When was it when I last saw you?" He chucked her under the chin. "At your christening, I think."

"That's right," said Mary Ann.

"Come on, come on in." He pushed them both before him, past the staring young lady at the desk, and the smiling elderly secretary, through the secretary's office and into a third room.

"Sit yourself down." He stood back from her and looked at her. "You haven't altered a scrap. You know, you never age, Mary Ann."

"Aw, I wish you were speaking the truth." She moved her head sadly. "I feel an old woman at this moment."

"Old woman? Nonsense." He waved his hand at her and pulled his chair from behind the desk to the side of it, so that he was near to her, and he sat looking at her hard before he asked quietly, "How's Lizzie?"

"Oh, she's fine."

"And Mike?"

"He's fine, too."

"And how's that big fellow of yours?"

Mary Ann's face became stiff for a moment, and then she said, "Oh, he's quite well."

Bob Quinton stared at her; then he looked at the child and smiled widely, and put out his hand once again and chucked her chin. And Rose Mary giggled just a little bit.

"Mr. Quinton, I've come to ask you if you could give me Mr. Blenkinsop's address. I . . . I understand you're going to build his factory for him?"

"Yes, I am, I'm very pleased to say." He bent his body in a deep bow towards her. "It's a very big contract."

"Yes." Mary Ann nodded.

"And you want his address?"

"Yes, please. If you would."

Bob Quinton narrowed his eyes at Mary Ann. There was something here that wasn't quite right. He had heard from Blenkinsop that he was putting the petrol side of the business in young Boyle's hands. He had intended to pay him a visit this very morning and congratulate him, yet here was his wife looking for Mr. Blenkinsop on the side. Why hadn't she asked Corny for the address? Mary Ann was a fixer; she had fixed so many people's lives that at one time he had attributed to her special powers. But the powers she had possessed were of innocence, the power attached to love, the great love that she bore her father. Yet the Mary Ann sitting before him now looked deflated, sort of lost. She didn't look possessed of any special power. He glanced at the child again; then, getting to his feet, he said, "What about a cup of coffee, eh? You'd like one?"

"I would, thank you." Mary Ann nodded at him.

"And milk for this lady?" He tugged gently at Rose Mary's hair.

"If you please," said Mary Ann.

"Come along. No, I don't mean you." He flapped his hand at Mary Ann. "I mean this young lady. She'll have to go and help Mrs. Morton fetch it."

He pulled open the office door and said, "Mrs. Morton, do you think you could take this young lady over to Simpson's and bring a tray of coffee?" Then leaning over towards his secretary, he said softly, "I would ask Miss Jennings to do it but I don't think I can trust her to bring the coffee and the child both back safely. What do you say?"

Mrs. Morton gave him a tight smile. Then, holding her hand out to Rose Mary, she said, "Come along, my dear."

Rose Mary hesitated and looked through the door towards her mother. And when she saw Mary Ann nod her head she gave her hand to the secretary.

Back in the room, Bob Quinton resumed his seat, and, bending towards Mary Ann, one elbow on his knee, he held out his hand, palm upwards, saying, "Come on, spit it out. What's the trouble?"

"Oh." Mary Ann looked away from him. "Corny. Corny and I have had a bit of a disagreement."

"Corny?" Although he had wondered why she hadn't asked Corny for Mr. Blenkinsop's address he hadn't, for a moment, thought the trouble was with him. Her da again, yes, because Mike, being Mike, was unpredictable. There had been some talk years ago about him carrying on with a young girl. But Mary Ann having trouble with Corny. Why? He understood they were crazy about each other. He remembered Corny from far back when, as a boy, Mary Ann had championed him. Surely nothing could go wrong between those two. But things did go wrong between people who loved each other. He had only to look at his own life. He said gently, "You and Corny . . . I can't take that in, Mary Ann."

"Nor can I." There were tears in her eyes.

"A woman?"

"Oh, no, no!" She sounded for a moment like the old spirited Mary Ann, and he smiled at her, then said, "What then?"

"Oh, it started with the children."

"The children?"

She nodded. Then, haltingly, she gave him a brief outline of what had happened, and finished with, "I heard yesterday he's going to sell out to Mr. Blenkinsop, and he mustn't do it, Mr. Quinton, he mustn't. He's worked and slaved, he's lived just to make the place pay, and now it's in his hands and it's going to be a big thing he's going to sell up."

"Well, you know, Mary Ann, I think the cure lies with you. You could stop all this by going back."

Mary Ann straightened her shoulders and leant her back against the chair, and then she said sadly, "He doesn't want me any more. If he had wanted me badly he would have come and fetched me."

"Aw! Aw! Mary Ann." Bob Quinton rose to his feet and flapped his hands in the air as if wafting flies away. "A woman's point of view again. Aw! Aw! Mary Ann. The medieval approach . . . is that what you want?"

"No. No, you misunderstand me."

146

"No, I don't. I don't. But you, above all people, I would have thought would have tackled this situation with reason. You, who have patched up so many lives, are now quite willing to sit back and watch your own be smashed up on an issue of chivalry, because that's what it amounts to."

"Oh no, it doesn't, Mr. Quinton." Mary Ann shook her head widely. "You're misconstruing everything; in fact, you're just like all the others."

"What, has your da said something similar, and your mother?"

"Everybody has."

"Well, I think they're right. But look; the time's going on and the child will be back in a moment. What do you want to see Mr. Blenkinsop for? To ask him not to buy Corny out?"

"Yes, that's it."

"Well, have you thought of the possibility that if he doesn't sell to him he'll sell to someone else?"

"Yes, I have. But . . . but if Mr. Blenkinsop makes it clear that he doesn't want to buy and that he won't give the business to anyone else if Corny goes then there'll be no point, will there, because he won't get very much for it as it stands, just what we paid. And we've hardly paid anything off the mortgage—you don't in the first few years, do you?"

A slow smile spread across Bob Quinton's face, and he moved his head from side to side as he said, "I'm glad to see that little scheming brain of yours can still work. And now it's my turn to act fairy godmother in a small way, because I'm meeting Mr. Blenkinsop in exactly"—he looked down at his watch—"twenty-five minutes from now. He's picking me up and we're going round the site. You know, I intended to look in on you to-day. . . . Ah, here they come with the coffee." He went swiftly towards the door and took the tray from his secretary. "And cakes! Who likes cakes with cream on?"

"I do."

Bob Quinton looked down towards Rose Mary as his secretary said, "She picked them."

"Well, she'll have to eat them," said Bob, laughing.

"I can't eat all the six. Anyway, Mam only lets me have one."

147

Rose Mary smiled towards her mother. Then, still looking at her, she added, "But I could take one in a bag for David, couldn't I, Mam?"

"Rose Mary!" said Mary Ann chidingly, and Rose Mary bowed her head.

It was half an hour later, and Mary Ann was sitting in the same chair, looking at Mr. Blenkinsop, and Mr. Blenkinsop was looking at her, and a heavy silence had fallen on them. They had the office to themselves, for Bob Quinton had thoughtfully conducted Rose Mary to the next room.

Mr. Blenkinsop now blinked rapidly, placed his hands together as if in prayer, then rubbed the palms one against the other before he said, "How did you come to know that I was going to buy your husband out?"

"Jimmy . . . our boy, he came round last night to the farm and told me. He . . . he thought I should know."

"Jimmy." Mr. Blenkinsop's lips were pursed, then again he said, "Jimmy." And now his eyes rolled back and he inspected a corner of the ceiling for a long moment before saying, "Well, well!" Then, rising from his chair, he walked about the room. When he came to a standstill, he said, "And you don't want your husband to sell?"

"No." She screwed her head round. "He's worked so hard, and he's doing it because . . . well, of what I told you . . . the trouble between us."

"He's a fool."

"What!"

Mr. Blenkinsop walked round to face Mary Ann. "I said he's a fool. He shouldn't put up with this situation; he should have gone to the farm and picked you up and taken you home and spanked you."

"You think he should?" Mary Ann smiled a weak smile.

"I do."

"You don't think I should have gone crawling back?"

"He shouldn't have given you time to do anything; he should have followed you straightaway, got you by the scruff of the neck and yanked you home." He was smiling as he spoke, and

148

Mary Ann, swallowing deeply, said, "You know, Mr. Blenkinsop, you're the only one who has said that, except . . . except his grannie. Everybody else seems to think that I should have gone back on my own."

"We . . . ell." He drew out the word. "Perhaps I'm used to dealing with American women, but under the same circumstances if their man hadn't come haring after them and grabbed them up and yanked them home. . . . We . . . ell."

"That's what a man would do if he cared for a woman, wouldn't he, Mr. Blenkinsop?"

"Yes. Yes." Mr. Blenkinsop suddenly stopped in his walking again. Then, thrusting his neck out and bringing his head down, he said, "Ah, no. Hold it a minute. Don't let's jump to conclusions. I'm saying that's what men should do, but we're talking about your man, and if he didn't do that then there's a very good reason for it. I've a very high opinion of your husband, Mrs. Boyle. I haven't known him very long but I take him to be a man of his word, a man of strong character, an honest man. Now a man with these characteristics doesn't stay put for nothing. Is there something more in it than what you've told me, eh?"

Mary Ann lowered her head. "Perhaps. It's a long story. It's got to do with the children. You see, he's always maintained that David would talk if they were separated, I think I told you. He's been on like this for a couple of years now. And Rose Mary getting lost proved him right, and we quarrelled, and I said something to him I shouldn't have done. It's that I think that has prevented him from coming to me."

"Ah, well now, if you know that you've put a stumbling block in the way of him coming for you, it's up to you to remove it, isn't it? Fair's fair."

Mary Ann rose to her feet and, going to the desk and picking up her bag and gloves, said, "About the business of buying him out, is anything signed yet?"

There was a long pause before Mr. Blenkinsop said, "No, no, not yet."

"Could . . . could you be persuaded to change your mind and say you don't want it, I mean say that you are not going to buy the place after all?"

"Well, seeing that he wants to sell, if I don't buy somebody else will, and that wouldn't suit my plans."

Mary Ann turned towards him but didn't look at him as she said, "You . . . you could say that if he sold out to anyone else you would stick to your original plan and put the buildings on the west side, Riley's side."

Mr. Blenkinsop's head went back and he laughed a loud laugh. Then, mopping his eyes, he said, "You should have been in business, Mrs. Boyle, but . . . leave it to me. . . . Mind, I'm not promising anything." He wagged his finger at her.

"Thank you."

"Well now, come along, I can drop you off at the end of the farm lane. How's that?"

Mary Ann should have said, "No, thank you, I've got other business to do in Newcastle," there was a job to be found, but she was tired and weary and so utterly, utterly miserable that she said, "I'd be glad of a lift."

It was about twenty minutes later that Mr. Blenkinsop halted the car at the end of the farm lane and watched Bob Quinton assist Mary Ann and Rose Mary to alight, and after the good-byes were said and Bob Quinton was once more seated beside him he drove off.

Mr. Blenkinsop drove in silence for some minutes before saying, "Well!"

"Yes, well," replied Bob Quinton.

"What's all this about, do you know?"

"About you buying Corny out?"

"Yes."

"I only know what she told me, that you're going to buy the garage and run it in your own company."

"Well! Well! Well!" The car took an S-bend, and when they were on the straight again Mr. Blenkinsop said, "When I go back to the States I'm going to tell this story like that play that is running, you know, 'A funny thing happened to me on the way to . . .' I'd better say on the way to a little garage tucked up a side-lane. Because, you know, I don't know a blasted thing about me going to buy him out."

"You don't?" Bob Quinton turned fully round in his seat.

"No, not a thing; it's all news to me. I did say to him jokingly, when I first told him of my plans, 'You wouldn't like to sell out?' and he said flatly and firmly no."

"Well, I'll be jiggered. But she said the boy, Jimmy, or some such name, the boy who works there, he came and told her last night."

"Yes, that's what she told me too. Well! It would appear that Jimmy knows more about my business than I do myself. Perhaps he's thought-reading, perhaps I do want to buy the garage. I don't know. But we'll find out when we meet Mr. Boyle, eh?" Mr. Blenkinsop glanced with a merry twinkle in his eye at Bob Quinton, and, together, they laughed.

A few minutes later they drew up outside the garage and Corny came to meet them.

During the last few days Corny had averaged a loss of a pound a day weight, this was due more to worry than to the scrappy meals he had prepared for himself. And only an hour ago he had decided he couldn't go through another day, more important still, another night of this. Whether she came back or not he would have to see her, talk to her before this thing got absolutely out of hand. There was a fear in him that it was already out of hand, the situation had galloped ahead, dragging them both with it. He had been saying to himself during the last two days what Mike had been saying to him from the beginning: why hadn't he stopped her, grabbed her up, brought her back and shaken some sense into her? But he had let her go; he had played the big fellow, the master of his house, the master of his fate who couldn't be . . . the master of his wife, the big fellow who couldn't keep his family together. He had reached the stage where he was telling himself that he had been to blame from the beginning, that he should never have suggested the twins being separated. Yet the truth in him refuted this, and he knew that he had done right, and the proof of this was now dashing round the place chattering twenty-to-the-dozen. Further proof was, his son had seemed to come alive before his eyes; he was no longer the shadow of his sister, he was an individual; the buried assertiveness that had at times erupted in temper was now verbal. There was no longer any fear of the boy being submerged by Rose Mary. . . . She could come back at any minute . . . any minute.

Last night he had sat in the screaming loneliness of the kitchen and wondered what Mary Ann was doing, but whatever she was doing, he imagined she would be doing it in more comfort than if she were here. She had never really considered this her home. That fact had slipped out time and time again. In her mind, home was still the farm, with its big kitchen, and roaring fire, and well-laden table, and its sitting-room, comfortable, yet elegant in the way her mother had arranged things. It seemed ironic to him that it had to be at the moment when he had prospects of giving her a replica of her childhood home that she should walk out on him.

He hadn't fallen asleep until after three o'clock, and he had been awakened at six by a hammering on the door. It was a motorist requiring petrol. That was another funny thing; he'd never had so much work in for months as he had in the last few days. Nor had so many cars passed up and down the road; it was as if the word had gone round. He had been thankful in a way that he had been kept busy during the day, yet all the while under his ribs was this great tearing ache.

A car coming on to the drive brought him out of the garage, and he now walked towards where Mr. Blenkinsop was getting out of it on one side, and Mr. Quinton the other. He nodded to each but did not smile.

"Hello, Corny."

"Hello, Mr. Quinton."

"It's a long time since we met."

"Yes, it is that." Corny jerked his head, whilst wiping his hands on a piece of clean rag. He brought his gaze from Bob Quinton and looked at Mr. Blenkinsop. The American had him fixed with a hard stare. He returned the stare for a moment; then said, "Anything wrong, sir?"

"Well, that's according to how you look at it. Can I have a chat with you?"

Corny's eyes narrowed just the slightest. "Yes, certainly." He turned and went towards the office, the two men following.

When they were inside there wasn't much room. Corny indicated that Mr. Blenkinsop should take the one seat, but Mr. Blenkinsop waved it aside, and, coming to the point straight away, said, "What's this about you wanting to sell out?"

"Sell out? Me wanting to sell out?" The whole of Corny's face was puckered. "I don't know what you're getting at, sir."

Mr. Blenkinsop flashed a glance towards Bob Quinton, and the two men smiled, and Bob said, "Curiouser and curiouser."

"You've said it," said Mr. Blenkinsop. "Curiouser and curiouser."

"Who said I was going to sell out? And who am I going to sell to?"

"I was informed this morning that you were selling out to me."

"You! . . . I don't get it."

"Well, to be quite frank, Mr. Boyle, neither do I, so I'd better put you in the picture as much as I can see of it. . . . I had a visit from your wife this morning."

Corny's mouth opened the slightest, then closed again. He made no comment and waited for Mr. Blenkinsop to continue.

"She came to ask me not to buy you out."

Corny's head moved from side to side, and then he said, "I don't understand. There's been no talk of you buying me out, has there?"

"No, not to my knowledge, but she had been told that you were going to sell out to me, and apparently this upset her. She knows how much stock you lay on the place and how hard you've worked and she didn't want me to reap the benefit." Mr. Blenkinsop laughed.

"But I don't see how. I've never said any such thing to her." His head drooped. "I suppose it's no news to you that there's a bit of trouble between us?"

"No, it's no news," said Mr. Blenkinsop flatly.

"Well, how did she get this idea?" Corny looked from Mr. Blenkinsop to Bob Quinton.

"Well, as far as I can gather," said Mr. Blenkinsop, "it came from you. You told your assistant, Jimmy, that you were going to sell out, and he goes and tells your wife."

"Jimmy!"

"Yes, Jimmy."

"He went and told her that?"

Almost before he was finished speaking Corny was out of the office door, and the two men looked at each other as they heard him bellowing, "Jimmy! Jimmy! Here a minute . . . in the office."

As Corny re-entered the office Jimmy came on his heels. He stood in the doorway, covered with oil and grease. You could say he was covered in it from his head to his feet. He, too, had a piece of rag in his hands, which he kept twisting round and round. He looked at the American and his grin widened; he looked at the strange man; then he looked at Corny, and from his boss's expression he knew that there was . . . summat up.

"You've been to the farm to . . . to see Mrs. Boyle," said Corny now.

"Aw, that." The grin spread over Jimmy's face and he said, "Well, I took the lads. You see, one of the fellows had set the piece she did, I mean Mrs. Boyle, to a tune."

"What are you talking about now?" said Corny roughly.

Jimmy again glanced from one to the other, then went on. "Just what I said. I went to the farm with the lads because of the piece Mrs. Boyle had written, the pop piece." He stopped, and again his glance flicked over the three men. And then he gabbled on, "She had the idea that if she wrote a pop piece it could bring in some money, and it could you know. It still could, it's good. Duke, our Group leader, he says it's good; he says she's got the idea. We're going to play it on Saturday night at 'The Well'. She got the idea because of what you said . . . sir." He nodded at the American. "You said she acts like a woman, you remember? An' I said to the boss here it was a good line, and so she worked on it and she said not to tell you." He was nodding at Corny now, and Corny said quickly, "Stop jabbering, Jimmy; that's not what I want to know. What else did you tell Mrs. Boyle when you saw her?"

The silly expression slid from Jimmy's face, and it was with a straight countenance that he said, "Nowt."

"Did you tell her that I was going to sell out, that Mr. Blenkinsop was wanting to buy me out?"

154

Jimmy now looked down at his feet. Then he looked at his hands and began to pull the rag apart. Next he looked at the men, one after the other; but not at their faces, his glance was directed somewhere at waist level. At last, after a gulp in his throat, he said, "Well, I . . . I did say that."

"But what for?"

Jimmy's head now came up quickly and, staring with a straight face at Corny, he said, "I thought it would bring her back, that's what. She knows what stock you put on the place. I thought she'd come haring back straight away. She's miserable, an' you're as miserable as sin, an' it's awful workin' here like this, so, well I got wonderin' what I could do, an' I just thought up that. But it didn't work. But . . . but how did you know about it?" His glance swept the other men again, and he chewed on his lip as the explanation came to him, even before Corny said, "She went to Mr. Blenkinsop here and asked him not to go through with it."

"Cor! I never thought she'd do that; I just thought she'd pack up an' grab Rose Mary and come haring back. I expected her to be here when I got in this mornin' . . . I'm sorry, boss." He was looking with a sideward glance at Corny, and Corny's voice was low as he said, "All right, Jimmy, you tried. I won't forget it. Go on."

The three now looked at each other for a moment; then Corny turned away and stood gazing out of the window while Mr. Blenkinsop said, "I wouldn't mind a factory full of that type."

"Nor me," said Bob Quinton. "It rather gives the lie to the thoughtless modern youth; at least, that they are all tarred with the same brush."

There followed another silence. Then Mr. Blenkinsop said, "You know, I feel very guilty about the situation; I feel I'm the cause of it."

"No, sir, don't think that." Corny turned towards him. "This started long before you came on the scene, and now it's up to me to put an end to it."

"You're going to fetch her?" asked Bob quietly.

"Yes, I would have done it before if I hadn't been so pig-headed. You climb up so far in your own estimation and it's a devil of a job to get down again." He looked from one to the other. "If you'll excuse me I want to get the boy ready; I'll take him with me."

"You go ahead." Mr. Blenkinsop nodded at him and patted his shoulder as he went out of the office, and then he looked at Bob Quinton and they raised their eyebrows at each other, and Bob said under his breath, "It's a pity he's been driven to do this."

"What? Go for her?"

"Yes; it won't do her any good in the future making him climb down."

"I know what you mean." Mr. Blenkinsop nodded. "Pity she couldn't have met him halfway."

Bob Quinton jerked his chin upwards and, nodding at Mr. Blenkinsop, he said, "That's an idea. That-is-an-idea."

"What do you mean?"

"Just a minute, I'll tell you." He put his head out of the door in time to see Corny taking David into the house and he called to him, "Do you mind if I use your phone?"

"Go ahead," Corny shouted back.

The next minute Bob was dialling the farm number. The phone had been switched to Mike's office in the yard and it was Michael who answered.

"Hello, Michael," said Bob. "This is Quinton here. Remember me?"

"Of course, of course."

"Look, I'm in a bit of a hurry. Is Mary Ann anywhere about?"

"She's over in the house."

"Could you get her for me? Or switch over to the house? You are on the phone in the house, aren't you?"

"Yes, yes, I'll do that. Hold on a minute."

It was some seconds later when Mary Ann said, "Hello, Mr. Quinton."

"Listen, Mary Ann. There's no time for polite cross-talk. I'm at the garage and as usual you're getting your way, Corny is coming over for you. . . . Are you there?"

"Yes." Mary Ann's voice was scarcely audible.

156

"As I said, you've got your way. I only hope you don't live to regret it; no man likes to come crawling on his knees." Bob Quinton jerked his head towards Mr. Blenkinsop as he spoke, and Mr. Blenkinsop jerked his head back at him.

"Oh. Oh, I don't want him to come crawling on his knees, I don't. Believe me, I don't."

"Well, you can't do much to stop him now; he's practically on his way; he's gone upstairs to have a wash and get the boy ready, and that shouldn't take him more than fifteen minutes."

"I . . . I could . . ."

"What?"

"I . . . I don't know. Oh, I want to come home, Mr. Quinton, I want to come home."

"Well then, what about doing it now?"

"But we'd likely miss each other. Anyway it wouldn't make much difference now because he'd think I'd only done it because you'd told me to. But . . . but I was going to come, I really was, I was going to come back after dinner."

"Look, listen to me. It's twenty-past twelve. There's the Gateshead bus if I'm not mistaken, passes along the main road around half-past. You and Rose Mary could sprint up that road in five minutes. It's only a fifteen-minute run in the bus to the bottom of the road here. It would be extraordinary if just as you were getting off the bus you should see the car coming down the lane. What about it?"

"Yes, yes." She was gasping as if she was already running. "Yes, I'll do that and . . . and even if I miss him I'll be there when he gets back. Thanks, thanks, Mr. Quinton."

"You did the same for me once. I always like to pay my debts. Get going, Mary Ann. Presto!" He put down the receiver, then passed his hand over the top of his head, and, looking at Mr. Blenkinsop, he said, "And she did, you know. She fixed my life for me years ago, and I have never forgotten it. . . .Well now, what we've got to do is to try to delay the laddie a little if he comes down within the next fifteen minutes. Have you time on your hands?"

"I've time for this," said Mr. Blenkinsop, "all the time that's needed. . . ."

Upstairs, Corny was saying, "Wash your ears. Wash them well now; get all the dirt out."

"Washed 'em, Da-ad, clean."

"Run and get your pants, then, the grey ones. And your blue shirt."

"Clean sand-ams, Da-ad?"

"Yes, and your clean sandals."

Corny scrubbed at the grease on his arms. The sink was in a mess; there was no hot water; he had let the back-boiler go out last night. He thickened his hands with scouring powder. It was like the thing. No hot water when he wanted to get the grease off, and she would go mad when she saw the state of the sink, of the bathroom, of the whole house. He stopped the rubbing of his hands for a second. What had he been thinking of? Why had he been so damned stubborn? He knew her; he knew she hadn't meant what she had said; he knew quite well that she'd had no real intention of walking out on him, that she had expected him to prevent her. Why hadn't he? Just why hadn't he? Looking back now over the interminable space of time since he stood on the road calling after her, he saw himself on that day as a stubborn, pig-headed, high and mighty individual. He saw himself on that day as a man still young, but he felt young no longer; the last few days had laid the years on him.

"Da-ad." David stood in the doorway, dressed in his clean clothes, and he looked from Corny down to his feet, and Corny said, "That's fine . . . fine."

"Goin' ride, Da-ad?"

"Yes," said Corny. "We're going to see your mam and Rose Mary." Corny did not look at his son when he gave him this news, but after a moment, during which David made no sound, he turned his head sharply. There stood the boy, his face awash with tears. The silent crying tore at Corny as no loud bellowing could have, and when, within the next moment, David had rushed to him and buried his face in his thigh he wiped a hand quickly, then placed it gently on the boy's head. This was only the second time he had seen David cry since that first wild outburst of grief when Rose Mary was lost, and it had been a similar crying, a silent, compressed crying, an adult sort of crying. There came to his mind the look he used to see in the boy's eyes when he was defiant, the look that had made him say, "That fellow knows what he's up to; he's having me on." He realized, as he stroked his son's hair, that there was a depth in this child, an understanding that was beyond his years. Perhaps it had matured because it had not been diluted by speech.

He bent to him now and said, "Come on. Come on. You don't want your mam to see you with your face all red, do you?"

David shook his head, then gave a little smile.

It was a full fifteen minutes later when they came down the stairs together, and Corny was not a little surprised to see that Mr. Blenkinsop and Bob Quinton were still about the place. But Mr. Blenkinsop gave an explanation for this immediately.

"You don't mind?" he said. "We've been looking at the spare piece of land, getting ideas . . . you don't mind?"

"Mind!" Corny shook his head.

"We would like to tell you what we think could be done, subject to your approval, of course. But that'll come later, eh?"

"Yes, if you don't mind."

Mr. Blenkinsop now stood directly in front of Corny and said, "How about to-morrow morning? . . . Is that all right with you, Mr. Quinton?" He looked at Bob Quinton; and Bob nodded, then said, "Hold on a minute. I'd better look and see." And then he proceeded to take a book from his pocket and study it.

Corny's eyes flicked from one to the other. They were blocking his path into the garage and the car. He didn't want to be brusque, or off-hand, but they knew where he was going, so why must they fiddle on.

"Yes, that'll do me fine," said Bob Quinton, glancing at Mr. Blenkinsop, and Mr. Blenkinsop, turning his attention again to Corny, said, "All right, will eleven suit you?"

"Any time, any time," said Corny. "I'll be here."

"Well now, that's settled. And now you're wanting to be off."

"If you don't mind."

"And we'd better be making a move, too. What about lunch? Have you any arrangements?" Mr. Blenkinsop moved slowly from Corny's path, and as Corny hurried into the garage he heard Bob Quinton say, "Nothing in particular, but you come and lunch with me. I have a favourite place and. . . ."

Their voices trailed away and Corny pulled open the car door and lifted David up on to the seat. A minute later he was behind the wheel and had driven the car to the garage opening. But there he stopped. You just wouldn't believe it, he said to himself; you'd just think they were doing it on purpose, for there was Mr. Blenkinsop's car right across his path and his engine had stalled. He put his head out of the window and called, "Anything wrong?"

"No, no," Mr. Blenkinsop shouted back to him. "She's just being contrary. Sorry to hold you up. She'll get going in a minute; she has these spasms."

Corny sat gripping the wheel. If he had to get out and see to that car he would go bonkers.

For three long, long minutes he sat waiting. Then with an exclamation he thrust open the door and went towards the big low car, and just as he reached it and bent his head down to Mr. Blenkinsop's the engine started with a roar.

Mr. Blenkinsop was very apologetic. "It's a long time since she's done it; I'll have to get you to have a look at the plugs."

"They were all right last week."

"Oh yes, I forgot you did her over. Well, it's something; she's as temperamental as a thoroughbred foal. I've always said cars have personalities. I believe it, I do."

Mr. Blenkinsop had turned his head towards Bob Quinton, and it seemed to Corny that Bob Quinton was enjoying Mr. Blenkinsop's predicament, for he was trying not to laugh.

"Ah, well, I'd better get out of your road before she has another tantrum. Sorry about all this." Mr. Blenkinsop again smiled at Corny, and Corny straightening himself, managed to say evenly, "That's all right."

He got into the Rover again and the next minute he was driving on to the road. The American's car, he noticed through his driving mirror, was again stationary. Well, it could remain stationary until he came back. But whatever was wrong with it, it didn't seem to be upsetting Mr. Blenkinsop very much for he was laughing his head off. Americans were odd—he had thought that when he was over there years ago—nice but odd, unpredictable like.

He turned his eyes now down to David, and the boy looked up at him, and they smiled.

When he rounded the bend he saw in the distance the bus pulling to a stop at the bottom of the road. He saw two people alight, a mother and child; he saw the conductor bend down and speak to the child; and it didn't dawn on him who the woman and child were until the car had almost reached them.

Mary Ann! Mary Ann had come back on her own. . . . Aw, Mary Ann.

He stopped the car and stared at her through the windscreen. She was some yards away and she, too, had stopped and was staring towards him. Then the next minute, as if activated by the same spring, they moved. Corny out of the car, and she towards him. They were both conscious of the children's high-pitched, delighted screams, but at this moment they were something apart, something separate from themselves. Eye holding eye they stared at each other as they moved closer, and when his arms came out she flung herself into them, pressing herself against his hard, bony body, crying, "Oh, Corny! Oh, Corny!"

"Mary Ann. Mary Ann." His voice was as broken as hers. He put his face down and buried it in her hair.

"I'm sorry. I'm sorry. Oh, Corny, I'm sorry."

"So am I. So am I."

"I shouldn't have done it. I shouldn't. I never meant it. I never meant to leave you; I must have been barmy. . . . I had to come; I couldn't stand it any longer." She lifted her streaming face upwards and simulated surprise as he said, softly, "I was coming for you."

"You were?"

He nodded at her, then said under his breath, "I've nearly been round the bend."

"So have I. . . . Oh, I've missed you. Oh Corny! Corny. . . . And home . . . and everything. Oh, I wanted to be home, Corny. I . . . I never want to see the farm again. . . . Well, not for weeks."

161

With a sudden movement he pressed her to him again; then said, "Let's get back."

They came out of their world to see Rose Mary and David standing, hand in hand, looking at them.

Both of the children now recognized that the gate into their parents' world was open again and, with a bound, they dashed to them, Rose Mary towards Corny, who hoisted her up into the air, and David towards his mother. Mary Ann lifted the boy into her arms, and he hugged her neck, and when Mary Ann heard him say, "Oh, Mam . . . Mam," the words as distinct as Rose Mary would have said them, she experienced a feeling of deep remorse and guilt.

Corny had been right. Her son was talking, and it was she herself who had prevented him from talking. She herself, who prayed each night that God would give him speech, had kept the seal pressed tightly on his lips; and the seal had been Rose Mary. And she had done it, as she knew now, not so much because she couldn't bear the thought of the twins being separated, but because she couldn't bear the thought of herself being separated from either of them. It was funny, the things that had to happen to you before you could be made to see your real motives.

"Oh, Dad. Dad." Rose Mary was moving her hands over Corny's face. "Oh, I've missed you, Dad. And our David. Oh, I have."

As the child's voice broke, Corny said briskly, "Come on, let's get back home." He put her down on the ground and put his arm out and drew Mary Ann to him; and she put David down, and together they went to the car, the children following.

A few minutes later they were back on the drive, and as they piled out, Jimmy came running down the length of the garage. The grin was splitting his face as he stopped in front of Mary Ann, and with his head on one side he said, "Ee! But I'm glad to see you back, Mrs. Boyle."

"I'm glad to be back, Jimmy."

Mary Ann's voice was very subdued and slightly dignified. He jerked his head at her twice. Then looking towards Rose Mary, he said, "Hello there, young 'un."

"Hello, Jimmy." Rose Mary ran to him and clasped his greasy sleeve, and he cried at her, "Look, you'll get all muck and oil and then your ma'll skelp me."

"She wouldn't. . . . Oh, lovely! We're home." Rose Mary gave a leap in the air, then swung round and grabbed David with such force that he almost fell over backwards; then she herself almost fell over backwards, metaphorically speaking, when her brother said to her, "Give over." Rose Mary stood still looking at him; then, glancing towards her mother and father, she cried, "He said give over. Did you hear him, Mam? A big word, give over, he said. David can talk proper, Mam."

"Yes," said Mary Ann, avoiding looking at Corny. Then she turned away and walked towards the house, and Corny followed her. And when Rose Mary, pulling David by the hand, came scrambling behind her father he turned, and, bending to them, said under his breath, "Stay out to play for a while."

"But, Dad, we've got our good things on."

"It's all right. Just for a little bit. Don't get mucked up. I'll give you a shout in a minute."

David pulled his hand from Rose Mary's and, turning about, ran back to where Jimmy stood. But Rose Mary continued to look at her dad. She wanted to go upstairs and get out of her good things; she had been in them far too long. Anyway, her dad should know that she couldn't play in her good things.

"But, Dad, it won't take a minute."

"Rose Mary! Stay out until I call, you understand?"

"Yes, Dad." Rose Mary remained still as Corny walked away from her and into the house; and as she stood, it came to her that their David had gone off on his own. She turned quickly about and watched David following Jimmy into the garage. He hadn't shouted to her to come on, or anything.

A funny little feeling came over Rose Mary. She couldn't understand it. All she could do was associate it with the feeling she got when Miss Plum, after being nice to her, turned nasty. The feeling spurted her now towards the garage. She was back home with her mam and dad and their David, and their David couldn't get along without her. . . .

163

Upstairs, in the kitchen, Corny sat in the big chair with Mary Ann curled up in his arms, very like a child herself. There was a tenderness between them, a new tentative tenderness, a tenderness that made them humble and honest. Mary Ann moved her finger slowly round the shirt button on his chest and looked at it as she said, "It's taught me a lesson. I don't think I'll ever need another."

"You're not the only one."

"Talk about purgatory. If purgatory is anything like this last few days I'm going to make sure that I'm not going to be a candidate for it. And you know," she glanced up at him, "they were awful. Everyone of them, they were all against me."

"Don't be silly."

"I'm not, Corny. It's true; even me da."

"Your da against you!" Corny jerked his head up and laughed.

"I'm telling you. As for my mother, I wouldn't have believed it. Even after she came to see you she made you out to be the golden boy."

Again Corny laughed. "Well, that's a change," he said.

"You should have seen the send-off she gave me when I came away. She was crying all over me. They all were, or nearly so. They were glad to see the back of me."

"Now, don't you be silly." He took her chin in his hands and moved her head slowly back and forward. "They took the attitude they did because they knew I'm no use without you."

She lowered her lids, then muttered, "You mean, they knew I was no use without you."

"Well, let's say forty-nine, fifty-one. But I know this much; they were all upset and they did their best to put things right. But it took Jimmy to do the thinking."

"Jimmy?" She screwed up her eyes at him.

"Yes. That tale about me selling out seemed to do the trick, didn't it?"

Mary Ann pulled herself upwards from him with a jerk and, with her two hands flat on his chest, she stared at him as she said, "You mean to say that was all a put-up job, you sent Jimmy?"

"Oh, no, no, no! Don't let's start. Now, let's get this right . . . right from the beginning, from the word go. I knew nothing about it until an hour ago."

Mary Ann was making small movements with her head. Then she asked softly, "You weren't going to sell out to Mr. Blenkinsop?"

"No, I never dreamt of it. Now ask yourself, as if I would, getting this far, after all this struggle. No, it was his idea. He thought . . . well. . . ." Corny lowered his head and shook it. "He thought it might bring you back and try to prevent me doing anything silly."

Mary Ann brought one hand from Corny's chest and put it across her mouth. "And I went to Mr. Blenkinsop and . . . and asked him not to buy you out, and. . . . Oh! Oh! I didn't only see him, I . . . I first went to Bob Quinton. Oh, what will they think? They'll think I'm batty."

"They'll think nothing of the kind; they've been here."

"No!"

"Yes. Now don't get het up. They wanted to know what it was all about. And that's how I found out that Jimmy had been to you with this tale."

"Oh, wait till I see him."

"Now, now." He took hold of her by the shoulders and shook her gently. "Think, just think, if he hadn't given you that yarn we might have gone on and on. There's no telling. Anything could have happened . . . Mary Ann." He bent his head towards her. "I just don't want to think about it; it frightens me; it frightens me still. I'm just going to be thankful that you're back." He smiled softly at her; then added slowly, "And take mighty good care in the future—you don't leave this house without me unless I have a chain attached to you."

He held her tightly; and as he stroked her hair he said, "And you won't go for Jimmy?"

She moved her face against him, and after a moment she said, "Fancy him thinking all that up."

"I've always told you that that lad has a head on his shoulders. There's a lot goes on behind that silly-looking face of his. And he's loyal, and that means a great deal these days. When things

165

get going I'll see he's all right. . . . You know, I could have kissed him this morning when he owned up to telling you that tale, and to know you still cared enough about me to stop me doing something silly."

Mary Ann gazed into his face, her own face serious now, as she said, "I've never stopped caring. . . . Corny, promise me, promise me that if I ever forget about this time and what's happened and I try to do anything stupid again, you'll shake the life out of me, or box my ears."

"Box your ears?" He pulled his chin in. "You try anything on, me lady, and I won't stop at boxing your ears; I'll take me grannie's advice and I'll black your eyes. 'You should have blacked her eyes,' she said."

"What! your grannie . . . she said that?"

"She did. And much more."

"But, Corny, she . . . she was the only one who was on my side; she called you worse than dirt; she . . . Oh . . . Oh!" Mary Ann bit on her lip to try and prevent herself from laughing. "The crafty old fox!"

"Ee! me grannie." There was a look of wonderment on Corny's face. "She's wise, you know."

They began to laugh, their bodies pressed tight again, rocking backwards and forwards. They laughed, but their laughter was not merry; it was the kind of laughter one laughs after getting a fright, the laughter that gushes forth when the danger is passed.

14

They'd had a meal; Mary Ann had cleaned up the house; she was now going to bake something nice for their tea; but before she started she felt she must have a word with Jimmy. She had just put the bread-board and cooking utensils on the table near the window when she saw him crossing the yard with some pieces of wood in his arms. Quickly she tapped on the window and motioned to him that she wanted to see him. In a minute she was down the back stairs and in the yard, and there he was, waiting for her at the gate. She walked up to him slowly and looked at him for a second or so before saying, "You should take up writing short stories, Jimmy."

"Me! Short stories, Mrs. Boyle? I couldn't write, me spellin's terrible."

"That doesn't stop you telling the tale, does it?" She looked up at him under her eyelids.

"Aw, that. Eeh! Well, I thought you would never come back. You see." He stooped and placed the wood against the railings; then, straightening up but still keeping his head bent, he gazed at his feet as he said, "You see, me mam and dad were separated for nearly a year once. Me mam always said it started over nothin', and neither of them would give in. Both of them were at work, you see, and me dad was on the night shift and we hardly ever saw him. Ships that passed in the night, he said they were. And they had a row, and she walked out. There was only me at home, 'cos me only sister, she's married. It was awful being in the house and nobody there, I mean no woman. I never forget that year, and so I felt a bit worried like about . . . about the boss and you."

"Aw, Jimmy, I'm sorry. I didn't know. But I'm glad you got worried about us. Thanks . . . thanks a lot." She put out her hands and clasped his arms, bringing the colour flooding over his long face, and for a moment he was definitely embarrassed. Then, his natural humour coming to his aid, he slanted his gaze at her as he asked, "It'll be all right for me to play me trombone then, Mrs. Boyle?"

She gave him a sharp push as she laughed. "You! That's blackmail. Go on with you."

He was chuckling as he stooped to pick up the wood, and she looked down at him and said, "I might stand for your trombone wailing, but I'll never stand for you having long hair like that crowd of yours."

"Aw." He straightened and jerked his head back. "Funny thing about that. Your dad got under Duke's skin a bit. My! I thought for a minute there was goin' to be a bust-up, but after we got back Duke began to talk about breakin' the barrier with a new gimmick, and he came up with the idea of shavin' their heads."

"No!" Mary Ann was covering her face with her hands.

"Aye, it's a fact. He's thinking of shaving up the sides and just leavin' a rim over the top here"—he demonstrated to her—"like a comb, you know, and callin' us 'The Cocks'."

"The Cocks!" squeaked Mary Ann, still laughing.

"Aye, that's what he says."

"Why not shave the lot off and call yourselves 'The Men'? That would break the sound barrier, at least among all the long-haired loonies. . . . THE MEN!" She wagged her finger up and down. "And underneath you could have 'Versus the rest'."

"Ee! you can think quick, can't you, Mrs. Boyle? That isn't half bad. 'The men . . . versus the rest'. I'll tell him, I'll tell him what you said."

"You do, Jimmy. Tell him I'll put words to all his tunes if they all get their hair cut."

"Aye, I will."

"Jim-my!"

"Ee! There's the boss bellowin'. I'll get it in the neck." He turned from her and ran with the wood towards the back door of the garage, and, as he neared it, Rose Mary emerged and, seeing Mary Ann, came swiftly towards her, crying, "Mam! Mam! Wait a minute."

"Yes, dear?" Mary Ann held out her arm and put it round Rose Mary and hugged her to her side as she looked down and listened to her saying, "Mam, it's our David. He won't do anythin'."

"Do anything? What do you mean?"

"Well, he won't play with me."

"Nonsense." Mary Ann pressed Rose Mary from her. "David won't play with you? Of course he will. Where is he?"

"He's with me dad, under the car."

"Under the car?"

"He wanted me to get under but I wouldn't, and me dad said I hadn't to anyway. Me dad told David to go and play on the old car with me, but he wouldn't. He waited till me dad got under the car and he crawled under with him. And they were laughin' . . . an' Jimmy an' all."

Taking Rose Mary's hand, Mary Ann said, "Come on," and with something of her old sprightliness, she marched towards the garage. David under a car! Thick with oil and grease! She had enough of that when she had Corny's things to see to.

Half-way up the garage, she saw Corny's legs sticking out from beneath a car, and next to the legs were those of David. His buttocks, too, were also in sight as he was lying on his stomach.

When she stood over the two pairs of legs she said, softly, "David, aren't you going to play with Rose Mary?"

She waited for a moment, and when no reply came she said sharply, "David!"

There was a wriggle of the buttocks and David emerged, rolled on to his back, stared up at her and said, by way of enquiry, "Mam?"

Mary Ann looked down at her grease- and oil-smeared son. She wanted to grab him by the shoulders, yank him upstairs, take his clothes off, and put him in the bath. She kept her voice calm as she said, "Aren't you going to play with Rose Mary on the old car?"

"No, Mam. Helpin' Da-ad." He held up one hand to her, and in it was a spanner.

Corny's voice now came from under the car, saying, "Give it me here, the big one, the one with the wide handle. Then go and play with Rose Mary."

"No, Da-ad." David was again lying on his stomach, only his heels visible now, and his muffled voice came to Mary Ann and Rose Mary, saying, "No, Da-ad, don't want to. This spinner?"

Mary Ann waited for Corny to say something. He had stopped tapping with the hammer. She could imagine him lying on his back, his eyes tightly closed, biting on his lip as he realized a new situation had arisen, a new situation that she would have to face. And not only herself but Rose Mary also. Her little daughter would need to be helped to face it, helped to watch calmly this severed part of her making his own decisions, choosing his own pleasures, living his own life. She gripped Rose Mary's hand tightly as she called in a light voice, her words addressed to her son but their meaning meant for her husband, "It's all right. Rose Mary's coming upstairs to help me bake something nice for tea . . . aren't you, Rose Mary?" She looked down into her daughter's straight face. Then, bending swiftly down, she called under the car in a jocular fashion, "But don't either of you dare to come up those stairs in that condition; I'll bring a bucket of hot water down for you to get the thick of it off."

"We hear." Following on Corny's laughing answer, David now piped in, "We hear. We hear, Mam."

Mary Ann moved away and drew Rose Mary with her, but all the way down the garage Rose Mary walked with her head turned over her shoulder, looking back at the car and David's feet, and she didn't speak until they reached the kitchen, not until Mary Ann said, "Go and get your cooking apron, and your board and rolling pin, and you can make some tea-cakes, eh?" And then, her lip quivering, she looked at her mother and said, "But, Mam, David doesn't want to play with me any more. Now he can talk he doesn't want to play with me any more."

"Of course, he does, dear. He's just new-fangled with the idea of helping your dad. That'll wear off. We'll go to the sands to-morrow if it's fine and, you'll see, he'll be like he was before. Go on now and get your things out and help me, because, you know, you're a big girl; you're six, and you should help me."

"Yes, Mam."

Mary Ann went to the table and made great play of setting about her cooking. New-fangled because he was helping his dad. Things would be like they were before. No. She was confronted with the stark truth that things would never be like they were before, for David had become Corny's; of his own choice, the boy had taken his father. As, years ago, she had taken her father and left her mother to their Michael, now David had taken Corny and left her to Rose Mary. Oh, she knew there would be times when he needed her, like there had been times when she had needed her mother, but it would never really be the same again. They might always be a close-knit unit, but within the unit one of her angels would fight his twin, and herself, for his independence. It was only in this moment that she realized that David was like neither Corny nor her; he was like her da, like Mike. He had been slow to talk, but now he had started he would have his say and fight for the right to have it.

"Mam, will I put some lemon peel in me tea-cakes?"

Mary Ann turned smilingly towards Rose Mary, saying, "Yes, yes, that's an idea; David likes lemon peel, doesn't he?"

"Yes, Mam. Mam, will I make my tea-cakes just for David and me?"

"Yes, you do that, I'll make some for your dad and you make some for David. That's a good idea."

Rose Mary smiled, then said, "Don't say I've made them until he's eaten one, then he'll get a gliff, eh?"

"All right. And make them so nice he won't believe you've made them."

"Yes, and he'll want me to make them every day. He'll keep me at it, and I won't be able to have any play or anything."

"Well, if he does," said Mary Ann, measuring the flour into a bowl, "you'll just have to say, 'Now look, I'll make them for you twice a week, but that's all, because I want to play sometime'. You'll have to be firm."

"Yes, I will." Rose Mary clattered her dishes on to the board, and after a pause she said, "But I wouldn't mind baking tea-cakes for David every day. I wouldn't mind, Mam."

"It wouldn't be good for him," said Mary Ann. "You won't have to give him all his own way."

"No, I won't."

Mary Ann turned to glance at her daughter. She was busily arranging her little rolling-pin and cutter, her knife and her basin, and as she did so she said, as if to herself, "But I wouldn't mind. I wouldn't mind, not really."

Mary Ann turned her head slowly round and looked out of the window. David, almost with one blow, had cut the cord that had held them together. He had flung it aside and darted away, as it were, leaving Rose Mary holding one end in her hand, reluctant to let go, bewildered at being severed from her root.

The plait of joy and sorrow that went to make up life was so closely entwined that you could hardly disentagle the strands. She wanted to gather her daughter into her arms and try to explain things to her, but she knew it did not lie in her power to do this; only unfolding years and life itself could explain, within a little, the independence of a spirit.

15

It was Sunday again and, outwardly, life had returned to normal; not that Corny's frequent diving upstairs was his normal procedure. Sometimes Mary Ann had never seen him from breakfast until lunch time, except when she took his coffee down, but now it seemed he didn't want to let her out of his sight. He came upstairs on any little pretext just to look at her, to make sure she was really there. It was a similar pattern to the first month after they were married.

But it was almost two o'clock now and Corny hadn't got back for his dinner. There had been a breakdown along the road and he had been called to see to it. She went into the front room and looked out of the window. She couldn't keep the children waiting much longer; yet Corny liked them all to sit down together, especially for a Sunday dinner. And she had made a lovely dinner . . . roast pork, and all the trimmings, and a lemon meringue pie for after. Rose Mary came into the room now, accompanied by David, and asked, "Is me dad comin', Mam?"

"I can't see him yet."

"Oh, I'm hungry."

"Me an' all," said David.

They were standing one on each side of her, and she put her arms around them and pressed them tightly to her. And they both gripped her round the waist, joining her in the circle of their arms.

She smiled softly as she looked down on them. Oh, she was lucky . . . lucky. She must never forget that. No, she never would, she assured herself. She thanked God for her angels and that everything in her life was all right again. . . . But not quite.

It being Sunday, and Jimmy content to stay on duty, they should have all been going to the farm, but there had been no mention of the farm to-day. Corny had remembered what she had said: "I never want to see the farm again. Well, not for weeks and weeks." And so he had not brought up the subject. Yet here she was, and had been all day, wishing she was going to see her ma and da and their Michael and Sarah, and sit round the big table and have a marvellous tea—that she hadn't had to get ready—and laugh . . . above all, laugh.

What was the matter with her that she could change her mind so quickly? A couple of days ago she had been glad to see the last of them. Did that include her da?

She bowed her head and released her hold on the children, and turning away, went into the kitchen.

She had just looked into the oven to see that everything hadn't been kizzened up, when Jimmy's voice came from the bottom of the stairs, calling, "Mrs. Boyle!"

She hurried to the landing and looked down on him. "Yes, Jimmy."

"The boss has just phoned from the crossroads to tell you he'll be back in ten minutes."

"Thanks, Jimmy."

"That's givin' you time to dish up; he wants it on the table." Jimmy laughed, and she laughed back. Funny, how she had come to like Jimmy. Before, he had simply been a daft youngster, but now she saw him in a different light altogether. She asked him now, "Will you have any room for a bite when I put it out?"

"Corners everywhere, Mrs. Boyle."

She flapped her hand at him and said, "All right, I'll give you a knock when it's ready."

"Ta, ta, Mrs. Boyle. . . ."

Twenty minutes later Corny was washed and sitting at the table and doing justice to Mary Ann's cooking, and every now and again he would look at her and smile with some part of his face. Then he would look at the children. He caused Rose Mary to laugh and almost choke when he winked at her.

After Mary Ann had thumped her on the back and made her drink some water, Rose Mary, her face streaming, said, "It was a piece of scrancham, my best bit, it was all nice and crackly. . . . Can I have another piece, Mam?"

174

"Yes, but mind how you eat it. Don't go and choke yourself this time."

After Mary Ann had helped Rose Mary to the pork rind she said to David, "You want some too, David?"

"No, Mam." David looked up at her; then immediately followed this by asking, "Goin' farm, 'safter-noon?"

Mary Ann resumed her seat, and David looked from her to his father, and Corny, after glancing at Mary Ann's downcast eyes looked towards his plate, and said, "No, not this afternoon. But we might take a dander down to your Great-gran McBride's."

"Oh, yes, Dad," put in Rose Mary, and both she and David made excited noises, interspersed with cries of, "Oh! Great-gran McBride."

Corny now said softly to Mary Ann, "All right?"

"Yes," she replied, but there was little enthusiasm in her voice. Not that she didn't like going to Fanny's, but free Sundays had always been reserved for the farm. She told herself that if she was strong enough she would say to Corny now, "We'll go to the farm." But it was early yet to face her family and the hostility they might still be feeling towards her; and this included Mr. Lord. She felt as if she had been thrust out by them all. The feeling touched on the primitive. As, in the dark past, some erring member of a tribe was cast aside, so had her family treated her . . . or so she felt; and the feeling wasn't lessened by the knowledge that it was all her own fault. . . .

Dinner over, the dishes washed, the kitchen tidy, Mary Ann set about getting the children ready before she saw to herself.

In the bedroom Corny was changing his shirt. He was in the act of pulling it over his head when he heard a car come on to the drive. His ear was like a thermometer where cars were concerned. He looked at himself in the mirror. When the cars began coming on to the garage drive thick and fast he felt his temperature would go up so high he'd blow his top. He was grinning at himself in pleasurable anticipation of this happening when he swung round on the sound of a well-known voice coming from the stairs, crying, "Anybody in?"

It was Mike. He was through the door and on to the landing

in a second, but not before Mary Ann, half dressed, with the children coming behind her.

They all stood on the landing looking down the stairs. Corny was exclaiming loudly, as were both the children, but Mary Ann remained quiet. She watched her father coming towards her, followed by her mother, and behind her mother slowly came Sarah, and behind Sarah, as always, Michael.

The hard knot came struggling up from her chest and lodged itself in her throat, and when her da put his arms round her shoulders she felt it would choke her. But when her mother, smiling gently at her, bent and kissed her, it bolted out from her mouth in the form of an agonised sob.

"Oh, there, there, child." Lizzie enfolded her as if indeed she was still a child, and she sounded very much like it at this moment, so much so that the twins stopped their gabbling and gazed at their mother. Then Rose Mary, tears suddenly spouting from her eyes, darted towards her, crying, "Oh, Mam! Mam!" And David stood stiffly by, his lips quivering.

"Aw, Mary Ann," Sarah lumbered towards her. "Don't . . . don't cry like that. We just had to come. I'm sorry if it's upset you."

Mary Ann, gasping and sniffing now, put her hand out to Sarah and shook her head wildly as she spluttered, "It hasn't. It hasn't; it's just . . . Oh!" Her glance flashed from one to the other of this, her family, and she spread her arms wide as if to enfold them all. "It's just that I'm so glad to see you."

Corny was standing by her side now, holding her, and he looked at her family, endorsing her sentiments, saying briefly, "Me an' all."

"Well," said Michael, who always had a levelling influence on any disturbance, "I don't like buses with standing room only. We're almost crushed to death in here, so if I'm not going to be offered a seat I'm going down into the garage to find an empty car. . . . And it's about time were were offered a cup of tea, if you ask me, we must have been here three minutes flat."

"Go on with you." Corny pushed Michael in the back and into the kitchen, and Lizzie, following Sarah into the bedroom to take off their outdoor things, shouted, "I'll see to it, Mary Ann, although it isn't fifteen minutes since they all had tea."

The children, returning to normal, followed their father and uncle. This left Mary Ann on the landing with Mike. Again he put his arm around her shoulders and, pressing her tightly to him, asked under his breath, "How's things?"

Shyly she glanced up at him. "Fine, Da."

"Sure?"

"Yes. Better than before, I think. I've learned a lesson."

"Don't we all?" He moved his head slowly above hers. "I've been sick over the last couple of days wondering, and your mother has an' all, and the others." He was referring to Michael and Sarah. "The house hasn't been the same; it was like something hanging over us."

Mary Ann moved slowly from the protection of his arm and went into the front room, and he followed her, and when they were quite alone he said, "You won't hold it against us for the way we went on? We only acted for your own good; we knew that you would never be happy away from him."

"I know, Dad, I know." Her head was drooping. "It seemed hard to bear at the time because nobody seemed to see my side of it, but now, looking back, I realize I hadn't much on my side, except temper."

"Oh, you weren't all to blame. Oh no." Mike jerked his head. "The big fellow's as stubborn as a mule. But, as I said, we knew that, separated, you would both wither. . . . You know, lass." He took her chin in his one hand. "In a way, it's the pattern of Lizzie's and my life all over again; except"—he wrinkled his nose and added quizzically—"except for my weakness, for I can't ever see you havin' to cart Corny home mortal drunk."

"Ah, Da, don't, don't." She turned her eyes away from him, and he said, "Aw, I can face the truth now, but as I was saying, the pattern of your life is much the same as ours. I knew I was no good without Liz, and he knows he wouldn't be any good without you; we're two of a kind, Corny and me. There's only one woman for us. There might be little side slips, occasioned by glandular disturbances in the difficult years." He pushed her gently and laughed, and caused her to laugh, too, and say, "Oh,

177

Da . . . Da, you're awful. Anyway"—her smile broadened—
"when Corny reaches his glandular disturbance I'll be ready
and——"

Mary Ann's voice was suddenly cut off by the sound of a band
playing; at least it sounded like a band, and it wasn't coming
from the wireless in the next room; it was coming from outside,
from down below on the drive. She almost jumped towards the
window, Mike with her, and together they stood staring down
at the four instrumentalists.

"In the name of God!" said Mike, then continued to gaze
downwards with his mouth open. Now glancing at Mary Ann,
he added, "Did you ever see anything like them in all your born
days?"

Mary Ann put her fingers across her mouth. "They've shaved
off their hair, nearly all of it."

"Shaved off their . . . !" Mike narrowed his eyes as he peered
downwards. "You mean to say that's the blasted lot that came
to our place the other night?"

Mary Ann nodded. "He said they might; Jimmy said they
might . . . Corny! Corny!" she called now over her shoulder,
and almost before she had finished calling his name Corny was
in the room, accompanied by Lizzie and Michael.

"What's all the racket?"

"Look at this."

"Aw," Corny leaned over her and looked down on to the
drive. "This is going a bit too far. I'll tear Jimmy apart;
you see if I don't."

"Corny!" Mary Ann gripped his arm as he turned to go.
"Don't . . . don't say anything to him, because . . . well, he
only tried to help me. You see," she spread a quick glance
round the rest of them now and said, "I . . . I wrote some words
and one of them set them to music; that's . . . that's what they
came to let me hear the other night."

"Well I never! Hitting the pops!" Mike was grinning now,
his attitude entirely different from what it had been a moment
ago. "And you wrote the words?" There was pride in his voice.

"Yes, Da."

"What are they?" asked Michael.

"Oh, I've forgotten; I've got them written down in the other room."

"Well, go and get them," said Mike now, "and we'll all join in. Listen to it! It's as good as you hear on 'Juke Box Jury'. I'm telling you that. Anyway, it's got a tune. What you call it?"

Mary Ann turned as she reached the door. "She Acts Like a Woman."

"She acts like a woman?" Lizzie was looking quizzically at Mary Ann, who, her face very red now, said, "It . . . it was something Mr. Blenkinsop said about me; well . . . about me going for Jimmy practising his trombone." She looked down and tried to stop herself laughing. "He said I acted like a woman."

"Well, I never!" said Lizzie. "And you turned it into a song?"

"Sort of."

"Well, go on; go on and get the words," said Mike, pushing Mary Ann out of the door.

It was plain that Mike was tickled and amused at the situation. But Corny wasn't amused; he didn't mind Jimmy practising now and again, but that was different from having that queer-looking squad doing a rehearsal on his drive, and a car might draw up at any minute. He turned from the others, who were now crowded round the window, and, running swiftly downstairs, he went past the instrumentalists and made straight for Jimmy, who was standing well away from the group and inside the garage.

Jimmy seemed to be expecting him, and he didn't give him time to start before getting in, "Now look, boss, it isn't my fault; I didn't ask them here. I told them not to start, but you might as well talk to the wall."

"SHE ACTS LIKE A WOMAN."

The group had become vocal; the voices soared now, and Corny, without speaking, turned and looked towards the performers. They had looked funny enough with their hair on, but now they looked ridiculous; their scalps bare except for a fringe of hair running from the top of the brow to the nape of the neck, they appeared to him like relics of a prehistoric tribe.

"SHE ACTS LIKE A WOMAN."

"Look!" shouted Corny above the falsetto pitch. "Drop it a minute."

Duke, his fringe of red hair making him look more odd than the rest, glanced towards Corny and said, "Why?"

"Because I say so," shouted Corny.

"You don't like it?"

"Look," Corny said, "we won't talk about liking or disliking anything at the moment. What I want to point out is that this isn't the place for practising."

Duke stared a Corny, and his eyes narrowed as he said, "I thought you were all right; Jimmy said you didn't mind."

"I don't mind Jimmy practisin' when he's got nothing else to do, but he'll certainly not do it on the main drive."

"Aw." Duke's head nodded backwards. "See what you mean. But do you like it? It's the thing your missus wrote. I had to alter bits here and there you know. . . ."

Corny rubbed his hand hard across his face, then said patiently, "It was very good of you to take it up, but look, go to the back." He pointed to the garage. "Go and play it there; you won't be in anybody's way there; then perhaps I'll tell you what I think of it."

"It's very kind of you, I'm sure." This cocky comment came from Poodle and brought Corny flashing round to say, "Now look, me young cock-a-doodle or whatever you're supposed to be; mind what you say and how you say it. Now"—he spread his hands out indicating the lot of them—"get yourselves through there before I change me mind."

The four boys went past him and into the garage; their steps were slow, and the glances they bestowed on him told him they were quite indifferent to anything his mind might do.

"For two pins!"

"Corny!" Mary Ann touched his sleeve, and he turned quickly to her. "I'm sorry."

Now he gave a forced laugh. "What's there to be sorry about? But you see"—his voice dropped—"I couldn't have them on the drive, could I?"

"No, no, of course not." She agreed wholly with him. "But I'm sorry that I ever thought about writing that bloomin' stuff."

"Don't you be sorry." He grinned widely at her. "They've made something out of it; they're going to play out at the back. Come on upstairs and let's have a look at the words and see how it goes."

"You're sure you don't mind?" Her voice was very small, and he became quite still as he looked at her, and after a moment he said, "I mind nothing, nothing at all as long as you're with me."

"Oh, Corny." Their hands held and gripped painfully for a moment; then they were out on the drive, their hands still joined, running towards the front door. But when about three steps from it, Mary Ann pulled them to a stop and on a groan, she said, "Oh no! Oh, no!"

"What is it?"

"Look down there. Am I seeing things or is that me grannie?"

"Good God! It's her all right."

"Oh, Corny. To-day of all days. And remember what happened when she was here last. Oh, Corny!"

"Look. Go upstairs and warn the others. I'll hold her off for a minute; I'll go and meet her."

Mary Ann seemed glued to the ground, until he pushed her, saying, "Go on, go on. You're not the only one who's going to welcome this visit . . . think of Mike."

The next minute Mary Ann was racing up the stairs.

"Ma! Da!" She burst into the kitchen where they were all gathered now, and, after swallowing deeply, she brought out, "Me grannie! She's coming up the road."

"What?" Lizzie, the teapot in her hand, swung round, "No!"

"It is. It is. Corny's gone to meet her."

Mike turned slowly from the window and looked at Lizzie, and Lizzie, looking straight back at him, said, "She must have gone to the house and found nobody there."

Mike moved further from the window. He didn't speak, only lowered his lids and rubbed his teeth across each other, making a sound that wasn't quite a grind.

"How she can come back here after the things I said to her the other day I don't know." Mary Ann was shaking her head when Mike said, "The one that can snub that woman won't be from this earth, lass; he'll have to be from another planet, with powers greater than any we can dream of; that woman's got a hide like a herd of rhinoceroses pressed together."

"Laugh at her."

They all turned their eyes towards Sarah, and she smiled her beautiful smile, saying, "It's about the only thing, failing a man from another planet, that will make a dent in the rhinoceros's hide." She was looking at Mike as she spoke.

"You're right. You're right." Mike nodded his head at her. "As always, Sarah, you're right. And that's what we'll do, eh?" He looked from one to the other now with the eagerness of a boy, finally letting his eyes come to rest on Mary Ann, and he added, "What do you say?"

"You know me." Mary Ann gave a quizzical smile. "I'll promise God's honour, and then she's only to open her mouth and say something nasty about Corny, the bairns, or . . . well, any one of you." She spread her arms wide. "You know me."

They all looked at her; there was a chuckle here and there, then they were all laughing, and at the height of it the group outside suddenly blared forth "She acts like a Woman". But even this combination couldn't drown Mrs. McMullen's voice as she came up the stairs.

No one went towards the door, and when Corny thrust it open and ushered the old woman in he did so with a flourish. "Look!" he cried. "It's Gran. I saw her coming up the road. . . ."

"All right. All right," Mrs. McMullen interrupted him sharply. "Don't go on. I don't need any introduction; they know me now. No need to act like a circus master." She moved forward, her glance sweeping over the crowded room. "Looks like a cattle market," she said. "Still, it doesn't take many to fill this place. Let's sit down."

It was Michael who brought a chair towards her; and when she was seated she looked directly at Lizzie, saying, "You could have told me, couldn't you, you were all going out jaunting? It would have saved me legs. But I'm of no importance; I'm young enough to trek the God-forsaken road."

"I didn't see any need to tell you we were going out, Mother; I didn't know you were coming."

"You know if I'm coming any day I come on a Sunday."

182

"It must be five weeks since you came; do you expect me to wait in for you?"

"No, I don't; I don't expect any consideration from anybody, so I'm not disappointed when I don't get it. . . . What's that racket out there?" She turned her head sharply towards the window. "What is it?"

"It's a group." Corny now walked past her and looked down into the yard before turning to her and saying, "They're playing a thing of Mary Ann's; she wrote the words. It'll likely get into the Top Twenty." He winked at Mike, who was standing to the side of him.

"Am I going to get a drink of tea?" Mrs. McMullen was again looking at her daughter—she was adept at turning conversations into side channels when the subject wasn't pleasing to her, and any achievement of her grand-daughter's was certainly not pleasing to her.

"Well, give yourself a chance to get your hat and coat off; the tea's all ready, just waiting for you."

Lizzie accompanied this with small shakes of her head that spoke plainly of her irritation, and Mrs. McMullen, after raising her eyebrows, folded her hands on her lap and bowed her head, and her whole attitude said, There now. Would you believe it? Would you believe that anybody could speak to me in such a fashion after asking them a civil question?

Then her head was brought up quickly by a concerted drawn-out wail and she cried, "Stop that lot! Who are they, anyway? And why do you let them carry on here?" She pulled herself to her feet and moved a few steps to the window and glared down on to the group, and its open-mouthed audience of Rose Mary and David.

All those standing behind her mingled their glances knowingly. Mrs. McMullen remained silent for a moment; then, turning her head over her shoulder, she looked at Corny and asked, "What are they?"

"What do you mean, Gran, what are they?"

"Just what I said: what are they? They're not human beings; don't tell me that; they look like something Doctor Who left lying around."

There was a splutter of laughter from Michael and Sarah, and Mary Ann, too, had her work cut out not to bellow, but on principle she wouldn't laugh at anything her grannie said.

"What are they singing? She . . . what?"

"'She acts like a woman'," said Corny, his grin wide now. "It's the title of the song Mary Ann wrote. Look, the words are here." He looked about him, and Mike, picking up the sheet of paper from the table, handed it to him with an exchange of glances.

"Look." Corny thrust the paper in front of Mrs. McMullen. "Read them; then you'll be able to sing with the group."

Mrs. McMullen's look should have withered Corny. She grabbed the paper from his hand and, holding it well from her as if it smelt, she read aloud, "She acts like a Woman. Man, I'm telling you she acts like a woman." Then only her muttering was heard until she came to the end. And now, handing the sheet back to Corny, she stared at him a moment blankly before emitting one word, "Edifying!" She turned about and resumed her seat; then repeated, "Edifying. Very edifying, I must say. But I'm not surprised; nothing could surprise me."

Mary Ann's face looked tight now, and Corny was signalling to her above the head of her grannie when that old lady explained the reason for her visit. She did it in clipped, precise tones, talking rapidly.

"Well, I didn't come here to read trash, or to look at four imbeciles; nor yet to listen to that awful wailing. I came to tell you me news."

Her statement, and the way she issued it, had the power to catch and hold all their attention.

"I've won a car," said Mrs. McMullen flatly.

There was a long pause before anybody spoke; then Lizzie said, "A car, Mother?"

"Yes; you're not deaf, are you? I said a car. An' don't look so surprised. Why shouldn't I win a car? There's no law against an elderly person winning a car, is there?"

"No, no, of course not." Lizzie's voice was sharp. "I was only surprised that you had won a car. But I'm glad, I'm glad."

"You won a car, Gran?" Corny was standing in front of the old lady. "What make is it?"

"They call it a Wolseley."

"A Wolseley!" The expanse of Corny's face widened.

"Do I have to repeat everything? A Wolseley."

Corny now looked towards Mary Ann; then to Lizzie; then his glance flashed to Mike, Michael and Sarah, before coming to rest on Mrs. McMullen's unblinking eyes again. Now he asked, "How did you win it, Gran? Bingo?"

"I don't go to bingo, I'll have you understand. No, I won it with a couplet for Pieman's Pies. A good couplet that had a real rhyme in it, and sense: 'Don't buy a pig-in-a-poke, buy a pig in a pie, Pieman's pie'."

Now the old lady's eyes flicked for a moment in Mary Ann's direction, and Mary Ann caught their malevolent gleam. Oh, she was an old bitch. Yes, that's what she was, an old bitch. A couplet that rhymed, with sense in it. 'Don't buy a pig-in-a-poke, buy a pig in a pie'. But fancy her of all women writing a couplet of any kind! She herself had sent in slogans for years; slogans for corn flakes, sauce, soap, boot polish, the lot, and what had she got? Nothing; not even a consolation prize. Yet here, this old tyke could win a car. There was no justice. It wouldn't have mattered if anyone else in the world had won a car with a couplet except her grannie, because her grannie was the least deserving of luck.

"And that's not all." Mrs. McMullen's head was now swaying like a golliwog's.

"Don't tell me you've won the chauffeur and all." This was from Michael, and his grandmother turned her head swiftly in his direction and said, "No. No, I didn't win a chauffeur, but I won a fortnight's holiday in Spain."

Nobody spoke; nobody moved. It would have to be her, thought Sarah. Why couldn't it have been my mam and dad? What use will she make of a car, or a fortnight in Spain?

Mike thought that the truest saying in the world was that the devil looked after his own.

Lizzie thought, "What is this going to mean?"

And Mary Ann thought, "I just can't believe it. It isn't fair."

And some small section of her mind took up her childhood attitude and asked what God was about anyway, for in dealing out prizes to this old witch he had certainly slipped up.

Corny, still standing in front of the old lady, said, "A fortnight in Spain? That's hard lines all round."

"Hard lines all round? What do you mean?" Mrs. McMullen picked him up even before he fell.

"Well, I mean you not being able to go to Spain, or use the car."

"What makes you think that I'm not going to use the car or go to Spain?"

Corny opened his mouth, straightened his shoulders, blinked his eyes, then closed his mouth as he continued to look at this amazing old woman. And she, staring back at him with her round dark eyes, said, "I'm going to use me car all right."

"But you'll have to get somebody to drive it," Michael put in.

"There'll be plenty to drive it, falling over themselves to drive it. Oh, I'm not worried about that. They'll break their necks for free jaunts."

"But where are you going to keep it?" asked Michael.

Mrs. McMullen now looked back at Corny, and for a moment he thought she was going to say, "In your garage," but she didn't.

"Outside the front door," she said. "Like everybody else in the street."

"A Wolseley outside the front door!" There was a shocked note in Corny's voice at the thought of a Wolseley being left out in all weathers.

"Why not? There's not a garage within half-a-mile of my street, and there's cars dotted all over the place. I've had an old wreck near my window for two years. And the Baileys across the road have just got a cover for theirs. Well, I can get a cover for mine."

A silence fell on the room again. Corny turned away. He didn't look at anyone, not even at Mary Ann, for the thought in his mind was: a Wolseley, a new Wolseley, standing outside a front door, subject to hail, rain and shine. It was too much for him.

"Did you win them both together, I mean the car, and the trip abroad?" asked Michael now.

"Yes, I did. It depended on how many points the judges gave you for the correct answers to the puzzle and the couplet, an' I got the highest."

"What are you going to do about Spain?" Michael had more sense than to say, "You can't go to Spain, Gran."

"I'm going."

"Don't be silly." Lizzie seemed to come alive at last. She swung round, grabbed up the teapot, went to the little tea table, and began pouring out the tea.

"That's a nice attitude to take, isn't it? I'm not in me grave yet."

Again Lizzie swung round, the teapot still in her hand. "I didn't suggest you were in your grave; but I do maintain that you're too old to go off to Spain on your own."

"Who said I was goin' on me own?"

Lizzie stood still now; they all stood still and waited.

"It's for two people."

Lizzie took in a deep breath, but didn't say anything.

"I suppose you think I can't get anybody to go with me."

"Well, I wouldn't bank on it," said Lizzie now. "Who's going to go traipsing off to Spain with . . . ?" She just stopped herself from saying "with an old woman". But Mrs. McMullen supplied the missing words. "Go on," she said. "Who's going to go traipsing off to Spain with an old woman like me? . . . And who should I ask but you, me own daughter?"

"Me!" Lizzie gaped at her mother. Then thrusting her arm backwards, she put the teapot on the edge of the table. It was only Mike's hand, moving swiftly towards it, that stopped it from toppling off.

"Now look here, Mother. Now get this into your head right away——"

"All right, all right, don't start. But I'm just putting it to you. Who's got more right to have a share of me success than me daughter? And on the other hand, who's duty is it to see to me but me daughter's? And there's a third thing. I remember years ago, years and years ago when you were young and bonny you saying how you'd like to go to Spain. You wanted to meet a Spaniard in those days. You thought the contrast with your fairness and his darkness would look well. Aye, and it would have. An, it's not too late; your life's not over yet. And if anyone deserves a holiday, it's you. A real holiday . . . a real one."

There was a movement behind the old woman as Mike went quietly out of the room, and now Lizzie, bending down to her mother, hissed at her, "Look. Now look, Mother. Don't you start on any of your underground tactics, because they won't work. I'm not going to Spain with you, now let that sink right in, and say no more about it, not another word." With this, Lizzie straightened herself up, glared at her mother for a moment; then she too went out of the room.

It was at this moment that the group down below, after having stopped, struck up again, and Mrs. McMullen, turning towards Michael with ill-concealed fury, cried, "Shut that blasted window or I'll throw something out on that lot!"

"The window's closed, Gran," said Michael quietly.

"Well, it doesn't seem like it." She looked round from one to the other. Then, turning her gimlet eyes towards the window again, she said, "You can't expect noise or anything else to be kept out of this little mousehole; it's a tunnel for wind and weather."

Corny planted himself deliberately in front of Mary Ann and swung her round and pushed her out of the door; and when she was on the landing she stood with her face cupped in her hands. She would hit her, she would. The wicked old . . . ! She wasn't really stumped for words—they were all there in her mind—but she wasn't in the habit of voicing swear words.

She walked slowly across the little landing towards the bedroom door; then came to an abrupt halt. The door was open and in the reflection of the wardrobe mirror she saw her ma and da. Mike had his arms around Lizzie and she had her arms around him. Mary Ann didn't turn away. Years ago she had joyed in watching such reunions between her parents—it meant that everything was all right—and as she looked at them the anger died in her. Mike's voice came to her softly now, saying, "I wouldn't mind, Liz. You can; it's up to you."

188

"Don't be silly, man. When I travel I'll travel with you or not at all. As for the Spaniard . . . I got him years ago."

Mary Ann turned away, and as she did so the kitchen door opened and Corny came on to the landing. "All right?" he whispered down to her.

She nodded and pointed towards the bedroom, and after catching a glimpse of Mike with Lizzie in his arms, Corny turned quickly away.

Taking Mary Ann into the sitting room, he said quietly, "Your world all right now?"

She nodded and dropped her head slowly on to his breast. Then she muttered, "Why couldn't I have won that car and the trip abroad instead of that old devil? I would have loved you to have had a Wolseley."

"Look." He took her by the shoulders and brought his face down to hers. "I don't want a Wolseley; I've got everything. I'll be so busy in a little while that I won't know where to put meself. As for money . . . well"—he moved his head slowly—"there won't be any more worries about that. Yet all that is on the side; the main thing is I've got you. You've always been all I wanted; you'll go on being all I want. I want you to get that in your head. Make it stick. You understand?"

Mary Ann's eyes were moist as she gazed up into his face. He hadn't mentioned the children, just her. She buried her head again, and he held her tightly. Then after a moment he said, "Do you know what? I know a way we could get her car."

She screwed up her face and he bent his head and touched her nose lightly with his lips as he said, "You could bring her to live here and I could garage——"

"Oh, you!" She punched at him with her two fists.

"Well, it's a way. I mean we'd be sure of the car. And just think . . . a Wolseley!"

"Corny Boyle." Again she was punching at him as he laughed. "Do you want me stark staring mad?"

His arms enfolding her once more, he rocked her backwards and forwards. "I want you any way . . . any way, Mary Ann Boyle. As long as you . . ." He released one arm and, throwing it dramatically upwards, thrust back his head and bellowed, "ACT LIKE A WOMAN."

"Oh, Corny! Corny! Oh, you're daft." She was shaking with her laughter.

"Come on," he said, hugging her to his side. "We'd better get next door and see the end of Dame McMullen's pantomime."

When they reached the landing, there was Mike and Lizzie coming towards the kitchen door, and Corny, taking up another dramatic pose, cried in an undertone, "United we stand, divided we fall. Forward, the Shaughnessy McBoyles!" And on this he thrust open the door and, with an exaggerated bow, he ushered each of them into the room. Mike followed Lizzie. Both were laughing. Mary Ann, following Mike, caught at his hand, and her other hand she placed in Corny's. She was happy . . . happy.

"Mam! Mam!"

"Ma-am!"

But when she heard her children call she released her hold on her father and husband, and, running back to the top of the stairs, she spread her arms wide to her angels. And as she held them she thought that it was odd but during the last few telling days, although she had not forgotten about her angels, they had been thrust into the background, and she had thought only of their father.

And that's how it should be at times; and that's how it must be . . . in the future.